"Leave You Alone?

You'd never forgive me if I did! This is what you want, isn't it?" He pulled her close to the hard wall of his chest and his mouth came down on hers with a bruising intensity.

For a long moment Barbara felt only anger and the need to resist him. But then her lips parted beneath his, and her body curled against him with the strength of her desire to get closer still.

"Try that trick again and you'll get more of the same!" he growled in her ear. "Only give me fair warning next time!"

"There isn't going to be a next time!" She answered in shaking tones.

ELIZABETH HUNTER

uses the world as her backdrop. She paints with broad and colorful strokes; yet she is meticulous in her eye for detail. Well known for her warm understanding of her characters, she is internationally beloved by her loyal and enthusiastic readers.

Dear Reader:

I'd like to take this opportunity to thank you for all your support and encouragement of Silhouette Romances.

Many of you write in regularly, telling us what you like best about Silhouette, which authors are your favorites. This is a tremendous help to us as we strive to publish the best contemporary romances possible.

All the romances from Silhouette Books are for you, so enjoy this book and the many stories to come. I hope you'll continue to share your thoughts with us, and invite you to write to us at the address below:

Karen Solem
Editor-in-Chief
Silhouette Books
P.O. Box 769
New York, N.Y. 10019

ELIZABETH HUNTER
Shared Destiny

Silhouette *Romance*

Published by Silhouette Books New York

America's Publisher of Contemporary Romance

SILHOUETTE BOOKS, a Division of Simon & Schuster, Inc.
1230 Avenue of the Americas, New York, N.Y. 10020

ISBN: 0-671-57240-7

First Silhouette Books printing August, 1983

10 9 8 7 6 5 4 3 2 1

Map by Ray Lundgren

America's Publisher of Contemporary Romance

Printed in the U.S.A.

Other Silhouette Books by Elizabeth Hunter

The Lion's Shadow
Bride of the Sun
A Touch of Magic
Written in the Stars
One More Time
A Silver Nutmeg
London Pride
Fountains of Paradise

Shared Destiny

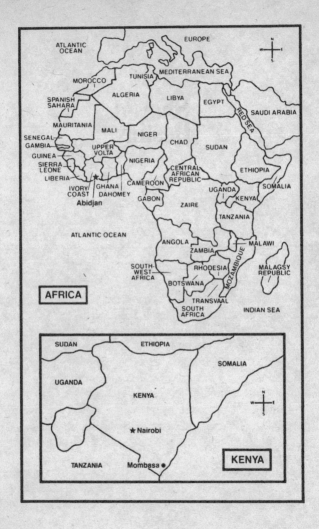

Chapter One

Away down below her the young Maasai swung his way through the bush, little clouds of red dust rising behind his sandalled feet like the spurs on a latter-day Mercury. In the rear came another man, helping a reluctant woman over the rougher patches. Barbara Nelson knew enough to decide that the second young man was the best man at the wedding and the man going ahead was the groom. She wondered how much of the bride's tears and pitiful reluctance was genuine and how much was playacting. Even Maasai women must want to get married, she supposed.

Bar Nelson had spent all of her early childhood on this land and, although she had been away from it for so long, she felt at home here as she did nowhere else. Europe had seemed so crowded and the people so old. Here it was possible to lean her back against a sun-warmed stone and look out across a hundred miles of wild land, with only the animals and those who still lived the old life amongst them for company. Here there were no cosy, well-ploughed fields, no patchwork scenery of hedgerows and tarmacked roads. Here the world was as it always had been, right from the time when man had evolved and had wrung a living from the very area where she was sitting now.

The Maasai wedding group came nearer to her, passing directly beneath the escarpment on which she was perched. She recognised the groom at once, remembering from the days when he had worked spasmodically for her father when he felt the need for money. More often he had followed the ways of his fathers, guarding the cattle allotted to his mother which would one day be his, standing storklike on one leg at a time, unconcerned by the passage of time.

He looked up and saw her, raising a hand in greeting. "You have come home?" he shouted up to her.

"I am at home," she agreed.

"Your father's spirit will rejoice!"

Bar hoped that was true. She had scarcely heard from her father in these last long years since her mother, hating the hot, dry land she had been brought to on her marriage, had taken her triumphantly back to suburban Britain, which to Bar, by contrast, had seemed everlastingly cold and grey. Her father had made no protest at her going. He had talked about the advantages of an English schooling and English values, both of which she had despised with all the vigour of a young girl approaching her teens.

"Good heavens, girl, you're not a Maasai!" her father had roared at her, exasperated.

Nor had she wanted to be. She had been brought up on the story of why the Maasai women did all the work in the tribe, their brothers reserving the rights to fight and herd their cattle but otherwise doing little but laze in the sun and gossip with their peers. Once the women had had their own animals to watch over, but they had neglected the task in favour of making a feast for themselves and the animals had been lost. From then on they had lost all the rights that the ownership of cattle had given them and had become the servants of their menfolk.

"I belong to this land as they do!" she had retorted.

Her father had merely looked sad. "I hope you'll always feel that way," he had said more gently. "You have to go with your mother now, but you can always come back when you're older. There'll always be a place for you here."

Bar stared across the valley towards Mount Lengai where the Maasai god was said to dwell, appearing to his followers at intervals in the rumbling thunder and the flashes of lightning that the mountain so often attracted to itself. She was home again now, but only because her father had been killed by the lion he had tried to turn into a pet, and she had come to claim her inheritance. Her father's partner hadn't wanted her to come. He had offered to buy her out, pointing out the impracticality of their sharing a house and lands. Stay in England where you belong, he had advised her. But Bar had never belonged in England. In England they told their children different tales and knew nothing of how to survive away from their safe towns and villages. They had never known the freedom of turning one's back on manmade things to share the life and instincts of the rest of creation for weeks at a time. In fact, they didn't see themselves as part of the same creation at all in Bar's experience.

Oldoinyo le Engai, the mountain of God, looked calm and welcoming. She hoped the old sky god was on her side for she was going to need all the help she could get. There would be no welcome home for her from Mr. Jonathan Grant, of that she was certain.

Reluctantly, she stood up to go. That Maasai down below hitched his terracotta robe more comfortably over his shoulder and went on his way, sneaking a look over his shoulder to see how his bride was progressing.

"My people will be pleased to see you!" he called up to her.

Bar nodded her appreciation, the tears coming into her eyes. At least she had not been forgotten. That had to be a good omen for her future. But then she remembered the closed border between herself and Mount Lengai, on which she had been pinning her hopes. Nobody could think of that as being a good omen for anything.

She could feel the approaching car in the throb of the land and wondered who could be coming her way. In the past, her father and she had always ridden out this way on horseback, and she might have hesitated to leave the main track if she hadn't seen that other tracks had gone this way before her.

She had bought herself a light Japanese four-wheeled-drive truck in Nairobi the day before, and she wanted a rest after the long drive to her father's farmhouse. This had always been a favourite retreat of hers and it seemed a fitting place to stop and eat the sandwiches she had brought with her.

A Landrover came to a scorching stop not far from where she was standing.

"Are you mad, walking about out here on your own?" a deep, masculine voice shouted at her.

She turned slowly to look at him, glad she had resisted the temptation to deck herself out in a tourist's idea of what safari gear should be. Instead, she was wearing a simple grey shirt, embroidered around the opening in a deeper grey, and a pair of trousers tailored in grey twill, which were smart enough to be worn in London, let alone right out here in the blue.

"You're never alone in Africa," she responded with lazy amusement. "Don't you know you have only to dig a hole for something to crawl out of it?"

There was a tremour in her voice that she hoped he would mistake for suppressed laughter. The truth was she had never seen anyone like him before. His pale green shirt and pants accentuated his toast-coloured tan and the bottle green of his eyes. His frame was tall and spare with muscles that rippled under his close-fitting clothes. His face was rough-hewn with a broken nose and a scar that cut one of his eyebrows in two. He looked well able to take care of himself in any society.

"What are you doing here?" he demanded.

"What are you?" she countered. "I'm at home here."

His hands tightened on the wheel. "You're Barbara Nelson," he accused her.

She inclined her head. "And you are Jonathan Grant?"

"Right. For your information, Miss Nelson, this is my home, not yours. If you'd wanted to claim an interest here, you should have come home when your father was alive. There's no place for you here now!"

She wouldn't quarrel with him on sight. But that didn't mean she didn't want to. Her eyes darkened with the dislike she felt for him. She was her father's daughter, wasn't she? And that gave her all the rights she needed to claim what was rightfully her own.

"Perhaps it's the other way round," she said quietly. "This is Nelson land you're on, Mr. Grant, and my name is Nelson, not yours!"

His mouth tightened into a straight line of anger. "You're out of date, Miss Nelson. You're standing on Grant land."

Bar's heart fell into her boots. "It can't be!" she exclaimed.

"Why not? Didn't you get your father's letter telling you I was his partner?"

"Yes," she admitted. "But I'm not willing to sell—"

"As I told you, you should have come home earlier. Why should you inherit anything from your father? Where were you when he needed you? Living it up in London at your father's expense? Celebrating your good fortune that he was finally dead?"

"None of those things." She hid her hurt as best

she could. "I think it's you who've got things wrong, and my solicitor agrees with me. Father's will said I had to be living in property owned by him to inherit. And I was! The flat in London belongs to him and always has done. He never made it over to either my mother or me, as she so badly wanted. He retained the title deeds right to the end. So put that in your pipe and smoke it, Mr. Jonathan Grant!"

He didn't seem to be as disturbed as he should have been. "I'll make enquiries," he said, almost mildly. "Meanwhile, you'd better come back to the house."

"My house," she said under her breath.

"Our house," he corrected her, looking her wryly up and down.

Bar wondered if his first impression of her was as devastating as hers of him. For once, she could almost wish she were as beautiful and soignée as her mother had hoped she would turn out to be, instead of being her pale and uninteresting self. She would feel better as soon as she had had some time in the sun, she promised herself, and rather less like some creature who made its home underground. She had never had any difficulty in getting a tan that was every bit as good as his and, having long, fair hair that she wore in a French pleat, the contrast between the two could be dramatic as well.

She glanced uncertainly in his direction and found he was still looking her over in that impertinent, mannerless way. Summing her up and finding her wanting, she thought with an angry sniff. Well, she was no Maasai girl to be bought for the price of a few cows!

"Finished?" she asked him caustically.

"Very nice—for London!" he approved.

"I belong here," she insisted angrily.

He raised his eyebrows and she was vividly aware of the scar that shone white in his tanned face. "I'd have more patience with that argument if you'd been the son and heir instead of the temporary heiress. Before you've had time to settle, you'll be married and off somewhere else. That's the difference between men and women, or haven't you heard?"

Bar gathered up her picnic things and threw them onto the back seat of her vehicle.

"Is that how you've squared your conscience for trying to deprive me of what is rightfully mine?" she challenged him. "Women stopped being men's chattels years ago. Get going, Mr. Grant, and I'll race you back to *my* house!"

She grinned happily to herself as she watched his dust disappearing into the distance. He had been her father's partner for years and yet he hadn't discovered her shortcut home, she was pleased to see. She would make it home first easily!

She set her own vehicle along the narrow track that ran along the very edge of the escarpment, travelling as fast as she dared. The last rain had been recent enough to have left the soil slippery under her wheels and, although she drove well, she had had no experience of driving in terrain such as this. It was as well that she was being careful, too, for ahead of her the track had fallen away, leaving a raw scar across the cliff, and she had to turn inland to find a way round the fall to where she could join the track again.

She had known plenty of similar falls in the past

but it was one thing to take a horse across virgin bush, and quite another, she discovered, to force a vehicle along the same way. The greening bushes tore at the steel sides, ruining the paintwork, and her unchained tyres were unsuitable for both the muddy and the dusty patches that caught by turn at her wheels. A troop of baboons chattered all about her, longing to put their thieving hands inside and snatch at her gear. She put up the windows and battled onwards, trying to accustom herself to their dropping down on top of her from a height whenever she went under a tree.

She would be a fool though if she allowed them to undermine her cool. If she wanted to be first at the house, she had to take every advantage she could get and starting out of her skin every time one of them came near her was not helping her make good time. She roared her engine and shouted at the greeny-grey baboons to stand clear. The vehicle rushed forward a few yards and then stalled. For a few seconds there was only silence and then the chattering started up again, followed by the sweet, bell-like calls of the birds.

It was then she saw the fawn, hidden away at the foot of a bush, its ribs sticking out at an angle indicating that it had been a long time since its last meal. Where was its mother? Bar looked all around her, forgetting her own fear of the baboons in the greater emergency the young gazelle was facing. It was not unknown for baboons to take and eat a young fawn if it came their way. In desperation, she tried to set the engine in motion again, but only a dull, scraping noise answered her fevered efforts.

An elephant crashed through the undergrowth close by. The baboons scattered out of the great animal's way, and at the same moment the engine sprang into life. Bar drove the vehicle forward, close to where the fawn was hiding. She opened the door, leaned out and attempted to grab the baby gazelle and drag it into the pickup, but she hadn't seen the young adult male baboon close by. With a cry, the baboon leapt at the open door, clinging on with its remarkably human hands, its mouth drawn back in a yellow-toothed smile of fright and anger.

It couldn't have been more frightened than Bar! She froze in sheer terror, waiting for the rest of the troop to attack her. Nothing happened. It was as if all life were suspended while the Creator himself drew breath. Bar stared into the baboon's sad eyes and was relieved when it was the animal that looked away, falling back to the ground and ripping at her shirt as it did so, leaving her almost naked to the waist. Bar clutched the shreds of cloth about her, glad that she was unmarked, for who knew what germs were trapped beneath the nails of that outstretched hand?

After that, it didn't take any courage to haul the gazelle up onto her knee. She put the fawn on the seat beside her, concerned by its blank eyes and thin condition. It swayed back and forth as though it were about to faint and Bar tickled it under the chin to give it courage.

"Somehow we have to get out of here," she told it earnestly. "Worse still, whatever we do now, that horrible man will be home before us! How are we going to explain that?"

How was she to explain the state of her shirt, come to that? She could only hope Jonathan Grant would have the sensitivity to be out when she did finally make her arrival at her father's house.

By the time she got back to the track the sun was setting. Mount Kilimanjaro, the highest mountain in Africa, was lit up in the golden rays, looking for all the world like a sagging steamed pudding in the distance. A few minutes later it was dark. She had become used to the twilight of a more temperate zone and was annoyed with herself for being taken unawares. Her headlights were inadequate for the terrain she was travelling, and every shadow seemed to menace her progress. It annoyed her even more to realise that she was frightened and that it was all her own fault that she was in this perilous situation.

It was hard to know whether she was glad or sorry when she saw other headlights coming towards her. Who else would be using this neglected track? Had Mr. Grant got tired of waiting for her and come to see what had happened to her? Her spirits sank at the thought.

He drew up opposite her, blocking her passage, and got lazily out of his Landrover, strolling over to where she was seated, clutching the wheel in front of her.

"I thought you'd come this way. Think you know everything, don't you? Are you prepared to admit this is no place for you after all?"

She clenched her teeth. "No, I'm not!"

He put his hand through her open window and flicked on the cabin light. Bar made a grab at her torn shirt, trying to cover herself before his interested gaze. If he were a gentleman, he would have looked the other way, but he did nothing of the sort.

"Are you hurt?" he asked her.

She shook her head, not trusting herself to speak. She put a defensive hand on the gazelle's head, trying to distract his attention from herself.

"Please go away!" she said crossly.

"My dear girl, if you are hurt, this is no time for false modesty. A mere scratch can turn into something very much worse if it's not treated at once."

"It's only my shirt—"

"Don't you wear anything underneath it?"

"Sometimes," she mumbled. Only it had been so hot that morning. She roused herself with difficulty. "Not that it's any of your business!" she snapped.

To her surprise, he grinned at her. "Very nice too!" he remarked. The scar on his brow showed up whiter than ever in the feeble light. "Are you up to following me home?"

"Of course," she said.

His glance was derisive. "You look fit for nothing! Bit off more than you can chew, didn't you?"

"Not at all!" Bar straightened her back and glared back at him. "I've always come this way on horseback before, but I could have made it home on my own. I would have been there by now if I hadn't stopped to rescue this fawn from a troop of baboons. *You* would have passed it by, I suppose?"

"So would you have done if you'd had any sense! It'll be dead by the time you get it home."

"Oh no!" Bar examined the tiny animal with gentle fingers. "It's breathing better than it was," she reported. "It's got used to my smell. I think it's only a few hours old. Once it's been fed and found somewhere safe to sleep, I'm sure I'll be able to persuade it to live. Won't I, my pet?"

"You're more like your father than I thought," Jonathan Grant said dryly. "Wild animals are meant to live free, not as pets!"

"All animals were wild once," Bar retorted.

"Some of them chose to be domesticated like dogs, some did not!"

Bar shrugged her shoulders, too tired to argue any more. "I'm not asking you to help bring it up, so why don't you mind your own business?" she asked him.

"Because it is my business. You won't be here long enough to finish the job—always supposing it does survive. You'll be back in London on the cocktail circuit before we can say Jack Robinson!"

Bar roared her engine, signalling to him to get out of the way. "That's what you think," she ground out. She had every intention of staying in Kenya until she was old and grey, and no Jonathan Grant was going to persuade her otherwise.

The house was smaller than she remembered it, but every bit as dear and familiar as she had left it. She got out of her vehicle and stretched tired limbs, longing for a hot shower and something to eat. An African came out of the house to greet her, a wide smile on his face.

"Memsahib *kajana*—no, not *kajana* anymore! Your father spoke of you often, but always as a little girl. He forgot that you'd be a grown woman by this time. It's sad he's not here to welcome you home, *mama* Bar."

Bar recognised the man at once and could have hugged him she was so pleased to see him. "Solomon! Now I've seen you, I know I'm home again! I rescued a fawn from some baboons on the way here. Will you help me feed him?''

Solomon approached the baby gazelle with the reserve most Africans have for all wild animals. "You should have left it where it was, *mama.*" He shook his head at her.

"I couldn't," she said simply.

"Like her father," Jonathan Grant put in behind her, getting out of the Landrover. "He'd be alive today if he hadn't made a pet of every wild animal that came his way."

"There's a difference between a baby gazelle and a grown lion!" Bar protested.

"So you say," Jonathan mocked her. "If it'd been a lion cub, you'd have brought it home just the same though, wouldn't you?"

"Probably," Bar admitted. She hugged the gazelle to her to conceal the gaping front of her shirt. "I'm going in to change. Am I in my old room?"

Solomon took her bags out of her vehicle. "It's just as you left it. Nobody has slept in that room since you left. Shall I take the animal, *mama?*"

Bar hugged it tighter still. "No," she refused.

"I'll take it," Jonathan said quietly, suiting the action to the word. He handed her his jacket in its place, effectively shielding her from the African's curiosity.

"Are you hurt, *mama?*"

"Not a scratch on me," Bar answered lightly. "I lost my shirt, that's all. I expect that wretched baboon thought—"

"Get inside!" Jonathan cut her off. "You can have your gossip when you're bathed and changed."

He made it sound as though she never did any-thing else but stand around and gossip. What was more, his coat was far too large for her and it was in danger of slipping off her shoulders and descending to her feet despite the buttons she had hastily done up. She turned to make her displeasure at his attitude more fully known to him, but he had already taken matters into his own hands by tucking the fawn safely under one arm and using his other hand in the small of her back to propel her into the house.

Her flesh burned beneath the heat of his hand and she dug in her heels to make him let go. "I'll go when I'm good and ready!" she said indignantly over her shoulder.

"You'll go now! Solomon has a woman of his own and isn't used to your London ways."

Bar turned and slapped him hard across the face. She had never done such a thing to any man before, and she wished she could recall the moment as soon as she saw the resulting red glow on his cheek.

"You shouldn't have pushed me! Leave me alone!" she whipped out.

"Leave you alone? You'd never forgive me if I did. This is what you want, isn't it, you little London alley cat? You're your mother's daughter all over again!"

He pulled her close against him, squashing her breasts tight against the hard wall of his chest, and his mouth came down on hers with a bruising intensity. For a long moment, Bar felt only anger and the need to resist him, but her lips parted beneath his and her body curled into his with the strength of a hot, urgent need to be still closer to him.

"Strike me again and you'll get more of the same!" he growled in her ear. "Only give me some warning next time."

"There isn't going to be a next time!" she answered in shaken tones. "I've never done such a thing before."

The look in his eyes mocked her, stilling her tongue. "Never? My dear girl, you can't fool me." He pointed her in the direction of her bedroom and gave her a gentle shove. "If you're wise, you'll keep out of my hair, or you might get more than you bargained for!"

To her, at that moment, it seemed the very best of all possible advice, and she was swift to take advantage of it, running away from him down the corridor as fast as her legs would carry her.

Chapter Two

The baby gazelle would need to be fed every two hours, Bar decided. She thought about asking Solomon to share the chore with her, but one glance at Jonathan from beneath her lashes decided her against that course.

Nevertheless, it seemed she was no sooner asleep than it was time to be up again, warming the milk for her small charge in the kitchen. The fawn had not taken kindly to being fed artificially. Bar had sacrificed her only pair of real leather gloves, making a hole in one of the fingers through which the animal could suck the milk inside. The small creature obstinately refused to suck.

Bar pushed the fawn up onto its feet, knowing that that was what its mother would do in the wild, supporting it with one hand. She talked all the while in a low, breathless voice, to give them both confidence, breaking into a lullaby the Maasai women had sung to her when she had been a baby. Somehow it seemed more natural than any of the other songs she knew.

"Tadotu dotu enginyi aaayai, (Walk, walk, walk, my little one),

Tadotu dotu enginyi aàayai, (Let us walk my little one),

Mapeepe teteyai mapéepe teteyai." (Slowly, let us walk slowly)."

The fawn took a tentative forward step towards the glove, and Bar gave it a delighted smile of encouragement.

"There, you see, you can do it after all!" she crowed.

A slight sound behind her made her turn her head to see Jonathan standing in the doorway, his arms folded across his chest, watching her.

"Why don't you speak to it in English?" he asked her. "It doesn't understand one language better than another, you know. Why cudgel your brains to remember something better forgotten?"

Bar's face burned with fury. "I hadn't realised I wasn't speaking English!" she exclaimed.

"No?" His disbelief made her angrier than ever. "Don't tell me your mother allowed you to learn the local languages?"

"What's the matter with that?"

"I thought her ambition was for you to be a little *English* girl, not a savage running around wild with the other savages out here."

"My mother was English," Bar told him in a strained voice.

"As is her daughter?"

Bar shook her head. "No, I was never English," she said simply. "I've never felt at home anywhere but here."

Jonathan bent over the animal, watching carefully as it winced away from his strange hand. "Singing it Maa children's songs isn't going to keep it alive. Has it taken any milk?"

"No," Bar admitted. "It doesn't understand what the glove's for. It took a little last time, but then it was sick. I'll have to try something else."

Jonathan grunted his disapproval. "Give it to me—and the glove. Some mother you make!"

Bar, already tired from her long journey and the adventures of the day, gave him a look of pure hatred.

"Let's see if you can do better!"

She might just as well not have spoken at all. Jonathan was completely sure of himself, and perhaps he had reason to be for he had excellent hands, coaxing the fawn to accept the support of his arm while he sprayed its small nose with milk from the hole in the glove.

"You have to tempt timid creatures to trust you," he said, his eyes on his task. "And try to remember that when they hit out at you it's as likely to be out of fear as anything else. They're not really too bright, you know."

Bar knew he was talking about her. She would love to have lashed out once more at his complacent face, but the presence of the fawn stopped her. She didn't know whether to be pleased or sorry when it began to suck, its eyes half-shut as its tongue worked round the leather finger.

"Oh, the darling!"

In her relief she put her hand on his arm and withdrew it hastily when she felt his hard muscles beneath her fingers.

"I'm glad you're pleased," he drawled, "but don't expect me to get up every other hour to feed the thing! That's your department!"

She nodded enthusiastically. "Let me try now," she begged. "He's got the idea now. Look at him!"

He transferred the fawn into her arms, putting the rapidly emptying glove into her free hand. "I think it had the idea before but the milk was too hot."

"The clever little thing!" Bar crooned to it.

"There's nothing clever about purely instinctive behaviour," Jonathan said dryly. "It wasn't in the least bit clever of you to hit out at me, was it?"

"You deserved it!" Bar told him firmly.

"No more than you deserved what you got!"

Bar sighed. "I'm not prepared to discuss it—"

"I'll bet!"

She turned her back on him, singing softly to the fawn under her breath as she did so. The glove was empty now and, with the suddenness of young things, the fawn slept, its legs crumpling beneath it, its head in the crook of Bar's arm.

"If we're going to share a house you'll have to get used to my seeing more of you than a stranger would," Jonathan went on, accenting his words with an undercurrent of laughter. "You've nothing to be ashamed of."

She was glad she was better covered now, even though she was in her nightclothes. She could cope with him now, she thought, whereas she had felt vulnerable and at a disadvantage before. We make too much of clothes, she told herself, and then remembered how he had caressed her, even while he inflicted that punishing kiss on her. Clothes were more of a defence than she had thought.

"Nothing at all," she agreed smoothly.

"I expect you've worn dresses in London that have shown even more of you if anyone cared to look," he taunted.

She was quick to reinforce her advantage. "I expect I have. We always go around half-naked in London—especially on the cocktail circuit!"

She saw the quick flash in his eyes and was satisfied. That round had gone her way, she thought in triumph. The next would be hers too if she had any say in the matter!

"Missing it already?"

Her moment of elation was gone. "What do you think?"

His eyes were hard as he answered. "I think you're very well accustomed to fending off male compliments—too well accustomed. Had a lot of boyfriends, have you?"

"By the dozen," she said calmly.

"You won't get round me that way."

She looked at him, forcing herself to look amused and a little superior, as though she had had her pick of any man she ever set eyes on. It was a hard task, because she had never seen one she liked the look of better than the one in front of her. He had a toughness of body that the men she had known in England lacked, probably because they worked in offices, as often as not by artificial light, and Jonathan lived in the open air and in a climate that had given him a skin the colour of toast and the look of one who was well accustomed to looking after himself in the wild.

"I keep telling you," she said gently, "it's you who have to get round me. This is my farm, not yours!"

His eyes narrowed, shutting her out of his thoughts. "I don't imagine that should be too difficult," he murmured.

A shiver went up her spine. "It's my farm!" she repeated.

"Is it?"

She tried to remember the exact wording of her father's will, but her mind wasn't functioning properly. She was tired, she thought, too tired to argue with him now.

"I'm going back to bed!" she announced crossly.

"Alone?"

Her breath went out of her body in a painful gasp. "Of course alone!" she almost shouted at him.

His lips smiled a very masculine smile, but his eyes were full of contempt that was somehow accentuated by the scar on his brow and his broken nose. "If you get lonely—"

"I've always slept by myself!"

He shrugged his shoulders. "Have you now? Do you really expect me to believe that?"

"Believe what you like!"

She flounced out of the kitchen, leaving him to settle the gazelle back in its box. How dared he? The heat of her anger coursed through her body, making her forget all about her tiredness. She felt more alive than she had for a long, long time. Sleep was the last thing she wanted at that moment! Then what did she want? she wondered, and was dismayed to discover she wanted to linger longer in the kitchen with Jonathan and convince him she was quite a different person from the one he had taken her to be.

Had her father been so disappointed in her that he had led Jonathan to believe he had fathered a jet-setter who had no time for the simple joys and virtues of the life she had had as a child? She wished she had kept in touch with him more, but she had had very little choice in her life style up to now. She had never wanted to go to England in the first place. Her parents had decided that her natural place was with her mother. Perhaps if she had written and told her father how miserable she had been living in her mother's shadow he might have done something about it, but children often suffer in silence, unable to differentiate between what is a fact of life and what can be changed. She had become a silent child with a cool exterior who had determined to get back to the land of her birth as fast as she possibly could.

Her mother had wanted her to be a social success. She had talked to her for hours about the kind of job she should get. Men don't like clever women, she had insisted, dismissing all thoughts of university for her daughter with an easy smile. But even more than men disliking clever women, they disliked girls who could think of nothing else but crops and the breeding of pedigreed farm animals. In vain had Bar protested it was the only career she was interested in, for her mother had been adamant in her opposition. To their mutual relief, Mrs. Nelson met a stockbroker at a time when Bar was secretly applying to the agricultural college of her choice, and her mother was too busy getting herself courted and wed to bother about her daughter's choice of career any further.

"Clive is willing to have you live with us until you marry, darling," she had said tearfully on her wedding day. "He'll introduce you to the sons of all the people he works with and you'll make a marvellous match. *You* won't have to waste your youth in a wilderness with a man who prefers wild animals to his wife and daughter! By marrying Clive, at least I'll have saved you from that!"

"I hope you have other reasons for marrying him?" Bar had returned uneasily.

"Well, of course. He has that lovely house in Sevenoaks—"

"Do you love him, Mother?"

Her mother's mouth had straightened into a tight line. "I loved your father and look where that got me. I can't imagine why people think that side of marriage matters so much, not if you haven't got anything else. I like Clive and he can give me the kind of life I've always wanted. Love is for children and for people who don't know any better."

It was a sad doctrine, Bar had thought. Sad and cold and the last thing in the world she herself wanted. She had never shared her mother's interest in material things. What she wanted was the sun and the smell of earth and growing things all about her, and to stand quite still and see a hundred miles in any direction at a time. It wasn't a cosy life she wanted, like the well-rounded hills and pretty countryside of England. She wanted grandeur and life taken straight from the hands of God, a life which was often uncomfortable, but always real. She would make a better tramp than a millionaire, she thought wryly. She had always preferred to walk than to go by car, and her stepfather's Rolls-Royce was nothing more to her than a car she found hard to drive because of its size and even harder to park.

Bar had not gone to live with her mother and her brand-new husband. She had made the usual excuses of not wanting to intrude on the newlyweds, which her mother had tried to dismiss as nonsense, but which Clive had greeted with something like relief.

"You're welcome for your mother's sake," he said to Bar. "If you took after her, it would be easier, but I think you must be more like your father. Truth to tell, it makes me uncomfortable to have you silently criticising me all the time. Why don't you like me? I work hard and I'll make your mother happy."

"I'm sure you will," Bar agreed warmly. "It's just that your money makes me uncomfortable."

"I came by it through hard work."

"I know," Bar said. "I admire you for it, but, just occasionally, I want to talk about something else, something that really matters."

He frowned uncomprehendingly at her. "Money matters."

"To you—and to mother it matters. It doesn't matter much to me, though, it never has."

"You've never been without it."

"True," Bar admitted. "But it's never brought me much happiness either."

"It bought you a good education. What more do you want?"

Bar smiled at him, trying to make him understand. She liked her new stepfather, much more than she had thought she would any man her mother would choose for her second husband, and she wanted to come to terms with him.

"You've never been to a girl's boarding school," she told him. "I hated every minute of it. To begin with, one was never allowed to be alone. One ate, slept, worked, and played with other people. If one was outside, one was told to go in; if inside, to go out! I guess you could call it culture shock, but it was very, very different from the life I'd been accustomed to. I never did get used to it. I want to go home to Kenya as soon as I can manage it. I don't want to be a foreigner all my days."

"An English girl should never feel a foreigner in England!" Clive protested.

"But I do," Bar convinced him. "I feel like that all the time."

There was nothing stupid about her stepfather. "I guess you do at that," he said at last. "But God knows how I'm going to explain it to your mother!"

Bar put her hand on his arm with easy affection. "As long as you don't think it's because Mother married you? I'm very fond of you both, but I could no more live happily as you do than fly!"

Clive bent his head and kissed her on the cheek. "I'll explain it to her somehow," he had said gruffly and Bar had wisely left it at that.

She had been right to come home where she belonged, Bar told herself now. She humped up her pillow and tried to relax her muscles to make it easier to fall into the slumber that eluded her busy thoughts. She only wanted what was rightfully hers. She wasn't depriving Jonathan of anything, for the farm had never been his in the first place.

Bar turned over onto her back. The native blankets on her bed had a smell she had long ago forgotten all about. It had always been there when she had been a child, she remembered now, the smell of African sheep, or perhaps the wool hadn't been washed in Western detergents. Possibly it hadn't been washed much at all. They were colourful though and rough against her fingers as she smoothed the blanket away from her face. Nor were the sheets much better. They too were roughly woven and badly ironed. She'd grown soft in England, she decided, if such things could matter to her now.

She hadn't minded the storm lamps at dinner, she comforted herself. It had always been a commonplace for the electricity to fail, often because her father had forgotten to start the generator in time. She had always liked the softer light of the lamps and the breathing noise they made. What she had forgotten had been how they attracted the insects after dark and, whereas she had been fascinated by their variety as a child, now she was discomforted by their determined dance with death.

Jonathan had changed for dinner, wearing a clean shirt and a sandy-coloured jacket that accentuated the tan of his face. He had taken the trouble to shave too, she noticed, and was glad she had donned one of her prettiest dresses, one her mother had bought for her, suitable for any and every occasion from afternoon tea to an informal dinner party. She had never thought of it as being cut particularly low until Jonathan set eyes on it.

"Very nice!" he remarked, making her wish it was done up right to her neck.

"I wanted to look nice for my first dinner at home," she said defensively.

He raised his eyebrows. "At home?"

"Why not? It *is* my home!"

"For the moment. That dress is revealing in more ways than one, my dear. It says where your true home is!"

The fun went out of her eyes. "My mother chose it," she found herself telling him. "Why do you have to be so unkind?"

"Unkind? I was just admiring the view!"

"It isn't your view to admire!" she snapped at him, cross with herself for being so self-conscious. She had worn far more revealing dresses than this one and had been complimented on her appearance in them, so why should she care what this man should choose to think of her?

"A well-trodden track?" he suggested dryly. "I shouldn't have thought you'd be so particular."

"I am."

He looked amused. "You must be very sure of your right to be here. What if the house, and the farm, belongs to me after all? Wouldn't it be as well to get on the right side of me?"

She hadn't deigned to answer, but sipped at the wine that was served with dinner. The venison stew took her back to her father's experiments with farming the indigenous animals, rather than the beef that had been brought in all around him. The wine was surprisingly good too, likely to go to her head if she drank too much of it—or was that the man opposite her?

"My father—" She broke off, too tired to argue

with him. "Were you here when he died?" she asked instead.

"I wouldn't have left him on his own."

Had she imagined the implied criticism she read into his words? . . . Bar turned her pillow again, longing for sleep. How could she have stayed with her father? What choice had she had as a twelve-year-old? . . .

"He told me he was bringing up a lion cub."

"She killed him."

Bar took a sip of wine to give herself time to think. "He must have been careless?" she said at last.

"He should have trained her to take her place in the wild instead of making a pet of her," Jonathan retorted. "I warned him how it would be!"

"I'll bet!" Bar flared at him. "You're always right, aren't you?"

He shrugged broad shoulders. "I know enough to know you can't tame a wild animal in one generation and turn it into a domestic pet. Sooner or later, it'll revert to the wild and turn on you, unless its spirit's broken and then it's good for nothing!"

"What really happened?" Bar asked, finding the silence that followed his words unbearable.

"She broke into the larder to steal a buck your father had shot that morning. Solomon was too scared to go anywhere near her and he went to get help. Your father grabbed her by the collar he'd put on her as a cub and she turned on him. He was dead by the time I got back with Solomon and the lioness was gone. We haven't seen her since."

"Poor Daddy," Bar mourned.

"He was a fool with wild animals. And you're

another one, bringing home that gazelle with you. If you do rear it, what will you do with it then? Fatten it for Christmas?"

Bar was shocked into silence. She must have been more tired than she knew because her lips unexpectedly trembled and her eyes filled with tears. How could she expect Jonathan to understand that the fawn was a symbol of her return to the world she loved? She set her chin at a stubborn angle and gave him back look for look.

"Why shouldn't I be a chip off the old block?" she challenged him. "He was my father, not yours!"

"You haven't shown much pride in the connection until now," he remarked. "I suppose your mother had more to offer you?"

"My mother's married again."

"So I heard."

"Was my father hurt that she should want to marry again?"

"You could have asked him that yourself?"

"I did," Bar revealed sadly. "He didn't answer."

"He probably thought you'd found a new father to look after you. It was years since he'd had anything to do with you."

Bar opened her eyes wide. "Clive? Clive could never be a father to me!"

Jonathan looked disapproving. "Like that, was it? Too bad you lost out to your mother." The insinuation was plain.

"Yes, wasn't it?" Bar answered defiantly.

Jonathan looked at her sharply. "Age before beauty?"

"Riches before freedom," she answered him.

"And which one did you want?"

She lowered her eyes before the look in his. "I'll leave you to work that out for yourself," she said and, rising, headed to the kitchen to see how her gazelle was getting on.

Solomon waved his arms at her, driving her firmly out again. "Don't you go handling that animal in the middle of your meal, *mama!* It'll wait till you've finished eating."

"Will it?" She needed reassurance that it was still alive to give herself hope that her own life on the farm would prosper no matter what Jonathan thought of her. "I only want to look at it, Solomon."

The African looked at her over his shoulder. It was hard to tell how old he was, but Bar noticed that his hair was quite grizzled. He was older than her father, she remembered, and an elder of his tribe long before she had been born.

"I'd say you need your meal more, *mama.* You're too skinny to be much use to a man."

Bar didn't mind the familiarity. She grinned at him, her eyes brightening.

"Englishmen like their women skinny," she told him.

It was unfortunate that Jonathan should have heard the remark. Why he couldn't have stayed where he was, instead of minding her business for her, was something else for her to worry about now in the long hours of darkness.

"I've lived out here long enough to appreciate a bit of flesh where it counts," he had said from the doorway of the kitchen. It was something, she supposed, that he said it in English and that Solomon probably hadn't understood him. It was something, but it wasn't very much. *She* had understood him and she hadn't liked his attitude at all.

"I wasn't talking about you!" she had retorted.

"Nor I about you!"

She would have given a lot to wipe the smirk off his face! She marched back to the table in the dining room and sat down, glaring at him. It would have been easier if he was a little less handsome, a little less sure of himself, and much, much less sure that he could get the better of her any time he chose.

"Sulking?" he asked after a moment's silence.

"Why should I, if you weren't talking about me?"

"You expect men to admire your figure—"

"I don't expect anything from you!"

He looked her over with exasperating thoroughness. "Solomon is right," he said at last. "You *are* too thin."

"It's got nothing to do with you!"

Laughter lit up his eyes. "What are you worrying about?" he taunted her. "You curve in and out in all the right places. That should be enough to save you from ever having to work for a living."

Bar became furious, furious with him, and even more furious with herself for minding what he said.

"I can't think why I bothered going to agricultural college and learning all about tropical farming if that's the case!"

"Is that what you did?"

She nodded. "I'm just as qualified to run this place as you are!"

"You lack experience," he had pointed out. "As to the rest, well, we'll see . . ."

Bar moved restlessly on the bed. It was almost

time to feed the fawn again. She pulled herself onto
her feet, trying to rid her mind of the image of her
father's partner, a man she could never, never bring
herself to like.

"I hate you, Jonathan Grant!" she said aloud. "I
hate you, hate you, hate you!"

Why then did she give two pins about his opinion
on anything at all? Why couldn't she just forget all
about him and *go to sleep?*

Chapter Three

Bar stopped the engine of her vehicle and listened to the sounds of Africa, leaning back against the seat with her eyes shut. What bliss it was to feel the hot sun on her bare arms and face and to know she could expect it daily for several months ahead, until the rains came to freshen the golden land that was all about her.

Some weaver birds had taken over a nearby thorn tree, covering every available space with their neatly made nests looking like so many minute baskets hanging from the branches. Bar listened to their chatter, amused to notice it was the males who did the weaving and the females who came along and picked their work to pieces again. She knew some human courtships that ran on much the same lines, her mother's for one. She had made many changes to Clive's house and home before she felt she could live in it herself.

Bar turned her head, knowing instinctively that she was being watched, and saw a single male lion sniffing the air close beside her. She knew she was quite safe in the car, but her heart began to beat faster as she gazed into the tawny eyes of the arrogant animal. She had always liked and admired lions in the past, but she had yet to forgive them for the death of her father. Jonathan could tell her it had been his own fault, but she couldn't quell an edginess that she'd never had before in their company. She wondered if, for the first time, she was afraid of them.

Lions are lazy animals and the large male soon grew tired of his speculation as to what Bar was up to on his patch of land. He stretched himself, circled once or twice, and lowered himself onto a patch of grass, squinting up at the sun, for all the world as if he were a domestic cat settling himself in front of a roaring fire in winter. Soon he was panting with the heat and waving his paws in the air to cool himself. It was hard to believe that one of his kind had deprived her of her father, just when she was coming back to him. Now she would never have the opportunity to get to know her father again. She would always see him through the eyes of the child she had been when her parents had parted company. It was a pity, because she thought they would have had a great deal in common.

She drove on to the Maasai settlement in the middle of the plain. She had always been forbidden to come here alone when she was a child. "A nasty, smelly place, her mother had said with distaste, I won't have you associating with them, Barbara." She felt an instant's guilt as she parked the car by the entrance to the *engang,* the family compound, because there was no one to stop her from coming here now. She had always been friends with the Maasai, the most dramatic of the tribes of East Africa, creeping out to visit them and as often as not relying on Solomon to fetch her home again without telling her parents. Solomon had always been her ally in all her escapades and adventures. He, too, admired the Maasai from a safe distance, because his was a quite different tribe. The Maasai never mixed with ordinary men, he would tell her. They had their own ways and their own gods and looked down on those who spoke other languages.

The compound smelt strongly of cattle dung and human bodies. Bar brushed the flies away from her face and went to the entrance.

"Hodi!" she called out.

The mother of yesterday's bridegroom came out to greet her. "I heard you're home," she said in Swahili, the *lingua franca* of all the tribes. "What have you to say for yourself?"

"My mother is well."

The old woman's eyes screwed up with some hidden joke. "You are fully grown yourself. Are you well?"

"I'm glad to be home."

"Ayee, your father is missed."

"By me most of all."

The old woman sniffed. "Have you no man yet?"

Bar shook her head. "No man. No children. I've come home to till my father's land."

The old woman snorted with laughter. "His land? What land does a dead man need?"

"It's my land now," Bar told her proudly.

"Tell that to the man who lives in your father's house!"

Bar didn't like to tell her that Jonathan's reaction had been equally caustic and unbelieving. Instead, she changed the subject.

"Tell me what you do now?" she prompted gently.

The old woman set her blanket at a more comfortable angle round her shoulders. Her nine-inch-wide necklace made of tiny beads threaded on stolen telephone wire flapped up and down as she moved.

"I am old and useless. Yesterday, my son Tikipit married a girl from a neighbouring encampment. He is too fond of her and despite all my protests he has given her the very best of all his cattle to keep for their son. That was my last task. What do I have to do now but gossip with friends and share my wisdom with the young women of the tribe?"

Bar made the usual long sound in the back of her throat that signified a mixture of agreement and an urge for the old woman to go on.

"Tikipit saw you when he was bringing his bride home. He said the man in your father's house would not be put off by your yellow hair. Tikipit knows these things. Is that why you came?"

To be Jonathan's woman? Certainly not! Bar sat up very straight and tried to stop herself from blushing.

"I am no man's woman!" she said proudly.

The old woman looked at her sadly. "I suppose they live a different life in the land where you've been if men and women have no need of each other."

"I didn't say that," Bar denied. "When I marry, I'll choose my own man. Meanwhile, I have the farm."

"How will you till your man's land as well as your own? You can't cross oceans daily to work the land of both."

"Perhaps he'll want to live here with me," Bar suggested.

The old woman cleared her throat and spat on the ground. "The ways of the white man are very strange," she commented. "You knew better when you were a child. Do you remember how you pleaded to have your two bottom teeth out as our children do? You said you were as likely to get lockjaw as they were! How angry your parents were! They forbade you to visit with me after that." She rocked herself back and forth, crooning under her breath. "You would have learned more sense if you'd stayed!"

"I thought so," Bar admitted.

The old woman laughed caustically. "You'll be old before you become a woman! What's the matter with the man who lives in your father's house? Have you a lover across the seas who won't let you go?"

Bar shook her head, laughing also. What else had a Maasai woman to look forward to but marriage and children of her own? It would be impossible to explain that there were other things in her life. The old woman would think them worthless, and she certainly wouldn't understand that Bar would only marry when she had fallen in love.

"An interesting question." Jonathan's voice came from the entrance to the compound. "Have you one lover, or was there safety in numbers?"

She sought in her mind for an answer, but the Swahili terms were so much more explicit than in English that she quailed at the thought of turning the question.

"Well?" he prompted her.

"It's a question without an answer," she said abruptly. "I spent all my time learning how to manage cattle and grow crops. I didn't have time for anything else."

The old woman moaned softly. "Ayee, child, you haven't lived at all! Such things are for men. Women are for the making of children and seeing that life passes from one generation to the next. They are the link between the past and the future and that must be enough for them. Isn't it enough for you to be the guardian of life?"

Not without love, Bar thought. Never without love. She switched languages from Swahili to Maa. "I have only tasted death," she said. "To be parted from all one holds dear is a living death."

The old woman was concerned. "Ay, me, daughter, what are you saying? The gods go with you wherever you go."

"But the sun doesn't shine much over there."

Jonathan took a step towards her, not liking to come right inside unless he was bidden. "All right, so you speak Maa," he chided her in English. "One up to you! I don't! What were you saying to her?"

Bar smiled at him sweetly. "Wouldn't you like to know?"

"Barbara Nelson, I've been trying to tell you ever since you got here that you're heading for trouble. You'd better keep on the right side of me!"

She put her head on one side, lifting her chin to a challenging angle. "Why?"

"It's up to me whether you stay or not—"

"Oh no, Mr. Grant. Nobody is ever going to send me away from my home ever again. Certainly not you!"

He was angry enough to strike her, clenching his fists at his sides and looking like a thundercloud. "I have the right—"

She shook her head. "You have no right to bully me over what is legally mine. Would you make all this fuss if I were a man?"

His anger fell away from him, leaving him amused and faintly contemptuous. "The fact remains you're not a man. It might be easier in some ways if you were, easier for me, if not for you, but it wouldn't be nearly as interesting—for either of us!"

The old woman looked from one to the other of them, chuckling to herself. "He looks angry enough to beat you if you don't do what he says," she pronounced in Maa.

"White men don't beat women," Bar assured her. "It isn't the custom."

"Don't be too sure of that!" Jonathan advised her.

Bar put a hand up to her mouth. Could he understand some Maa after all? But no, she had been foolish enough to speak in Swahili, which came much more easily to her tongue.

The old woman cackled a laugh. "He's a man, daughter, take him while you can!"

Bar felt herself colour up, although Jonathan had no way of understanding what the old woman had said. He was a man, she thought. More of a man than any other she had ever met. He had only to look at her and she knew herself to be wholly female too. Nobody else had ever had that effect on her either. He was far more of a danger to her plans for the future than she wanted to admit. She simply didn't know what to do about him, not until she knew what her father had intended for his future. Even if she turned out to be the sole owner of the farm, would she want to turn him away?

"I can wait," she said in Maa.

"But will he?"

Jonathan's baffled expression made both women break into easy laughter. It was strange, Bar thought, that no matter how remote their lives women could always find a bond in common, discussing men and children and the difficulties of keeping house whether it was in the suburbs or the wilderness. The thought brought a sparkle to her eyes as she turned them onto Jonathan, knowing he would think they were laughing at him.

"Did you want me?" she asked him.

His own lips curved into a smile. "It's an interesting thought."

"An interesting thought, an interesting question!" she scoffed. "You must have followed me here for something?"

"You might not like the answer if I gave it to you," he warned her.

"I'll risk it."

His smile deepened. "I could say I had designs on

your virtue, but actually I've come to take you over to visit the Allans. Remember them?"

"Indeed I do." She was glad to be seeing them again. She remembered them as a kindly couple who, partly because they were also the nearest European neighbours, had been her parents' best friends when she was a child. Their son she had seen frequently in England, but it would be nice to see the older couple again. "I was going over to see them this afternoon. I'm visiting all my old friends this afternoon."

"They heard you were back," Jonathan said slowly.

"You mean you told them!"

"I thought it wiser. I thought they might put you up for a while."

"Me?" She stared at him blankly. "Why?"

"They don't think you ought to be sharing a roof with me. I don't either."

Bar swung herself up onto her feet. "Then when are you moving out?" she demanded.

"You are!"

She clenched her teeth, her worst suspicions about him confirmed. "They wouldn't have thought about it if you hadn't put the idea into their heads! And you needn't think I'm moving anywhere! It's my house and my farm and here I'm staying!"

"Tell them about it," he invited her calmly.

"I will!"

He gestured towards her car. "Good. Then shall we go?"

But Bar was in no hurry to go anywhere with him. She drew out the endless, polite phrases of farewell as long as she dared, eyeing him covertly through her lashes. He showed no signs of impatience at her tactics, merely flicking at his boots with his flywhisk. It was the most beautiful flywhisk she had ever seen, and she longed to ask him who had made it for him. She told herself it would be bad tactics to admire anything of his, and so she frowned instead, hitting out at the flies with her hand as she did so.

"Aren't you going to say goodbye?" she needled him deliberately. "No wonder they say white people have no manners!"

He turned and looked fully at her then. "Maasai men don't speak to women unless they belong to them. Are you coming, or not?"

"I'm coming," she said.

Mrs. Allan was exactly as Bar remembered her. A wiry, petite woman, she had become a part of the Africa Bar had always loved. Mrs. Allan was at home here, taking all political and social changes in her stride, a better farmer than her husband, who never expected more of either animals or people than was theirs to give.

"I am so glad to see you!" Bar exclaimed, hugging her.

"You were away far too long," the older woman said.

"Yes," Bar agreed sadly.

"It was the way he would have wanted to die," Mrs. Allan pointed out.

"It seems such a waste," Bar sighed. "Why take such a risk, no matter how well he thought he knew the animal?"

"It doesn't do to trust wild animals, they don't know their own strength. I worry about that beast, alone in a strange world. Your father should have prepared her for eventual freedom, not raised her like a dog."

"He loved her."

Mrs. Allan twisted her lips into a grimace of disapproval. "He needed something to love, but that isn't the same thing. Lions aren't people to be house-trained because a man is lonely for company."

Bar immediately felt guilty at staying away so long. "He knew I was coming as soon as I'd finished at college. Why couldn't he have waited?"

"I don't think he thought you'd stay," Mrs. Allan said gently. "He thought London could offer you a better and more varied life. He hoped you'd marry—"

"Never in England!" Bar maintained stubbornly.

She followed her hostess into the kitchen to help her make tea for when the two men deigned to come inside and join them.

"It's ironic, isn't it? I never wanted anything more than to live on my father's land in my father's house. It's the only place I've ever been happy. Yet both my parents were convinced it would be better for me to be elsewhere, first at a school I hated, and then staying on in England in a kind of limbo. Clive, my stepfather, rescued me from that, or I probably wouldn't be here now. Only his refusal to have me living with him and Mother made my father offer me shelter. Can you believe that? But then you really want your son out here with you—remember how proud you were of Michael when he went out herding the cattle when he was small?—and all he wants is to live as far away from here as possible, in his university in England."

"He's welcome to his own life, dear."

"Don't you want him to take over here eventually?" Bar probed.

"Not if he doesn't want to. To tell the truth, I always thought it a mistake not to allow you to come to your father for visits, but I do know he suggested it to your mother more than once. She hated it out here so much herself, though, that she couldn't believe you really wanted to come. She really did hate it, every moment of every day. She was afraid of the animals and of the people. Up to a point I agree with her, too. Nobody should live here who hates it that much. We've had far too many people here who pine to do their shopping in an English high street. Nice people, but they don't transplant out of their own soil. Your mother was like that."

"I know," said Bar. "She loves where she's living now."

Mrs. Allan eyed her shrewdly. "And you?"

"I felt stifled."

"Then you don't want to go back there?"

Bar shook her head violently. "Fortunately I don't have to! The farm's mine now."

"Doesn't Jonathan have a share?"

Bar gave her an uncomfortable look. "I'm not sure. I'm not sure how things stood between him and Father. It's been rather difficult to ask him because he hasn't been exactly welcoming—"

"Did you expect him to be?"

"I never gave him a thought," Bar admitted carelessly. Her mouth set in a stubborn line. "I think he wants to do me out of the house and the farm!"

"He's worked hard."

"So have I!"

"I'm sure you have. It might have been easier all round if you'd come home the moment you were twenty-one though. Your father talked about nothing else for months. Couldn't you have come for a visit then?"

"I wanted to," Bar confessed. "Mother made me promise to finish at college first and I thought I owed her that. We both knew I'd make my home here as soon as I could, only she didn't want to admit it. I hated to hurt her, but she has Clive now. He's exactly right for her."

Mrs. Allan busied herself making the tea. "It must have been hard for you to go against her wishes. Michael said you had to fight like mad to get to agricultural college. He admired you for it."

"That was the easy bit," Bar said wryly. "The hard bit was telling her that I was coming out here. Clive told her in the end. You'd have thought I was going to Outer Mongolia."

"As far as she was concerned you were!"

"Well, yes," Bar admitted. "I love her dearly, but I've never been able to understand why she hated living here so much. She loved Father, so it wasn't that. All she would say was that it never rained properly and she couldn't have coffee with her friends. She used to come and have tea with you all the time."

"So she did," Mrs. Allan agreed. "She could

hardly dress up to come and see me though, could she?"

Bar chuckled at the thought. "I suppose not. It's so good to see you again! I wish Father—" She broke off, her face clouding over. "Jonathan said you'd invited me to stay here with you?"

Mrs. Allan picked up the tray, leaving Bar to follow with the teapot. "Don't you want to?"

"I feel I have to stand my ground. Once he gets me out, he'll find a hundred and one reasons not to let me into my own house! I'm sure he believes in possession being nine-tenths of the law. So do I!"

"I see."

Bar gave her hostess a suspicious look. "What does that mean?" she demanded.

"I was wondering if you'd really thought this thing through. Your father was on his own for five years after your mother left, but Jonathan has been his partner and lived with him there for the last five. He was like a son to your father. That house is his home, Barbara. It hasn't been that to you, has it, for the last ten years?"

"Nor has anywhere else!"

Mrs. Allan smiled sympathetically. "I understand that, my dear, but try to look at things from Jonathan's point of view. He's had every reason to think the farm would be his—perhaps it is his partly, your father always referred to him as his partner—and now he's about to be married, how is he to explain your presence in the house to his girl friend?"

Bar registered the shock of Jonathan being married to anyone the whole way down her spine. She didn't know why she should care. She hardly knew him, and what she did know she didn't like! What did it matter to her that he was in love and about to be married?

Was it the way he had kissed her? She felt a sudden tightening in her throat, remembering the arrogant way he had handled her on that occasion.

"If he's getting married, he'll have to build his own house!"

Mrs. Allan looked uncertain. "If I were you, I'd go to Nairobi and find out from your father's solicitor exactly what both your positions are. Meanwhile, if you want to stay here, you're more than welcome."

"Thank you, but no."

Bar sounded a great deal more definite than she felt. She didn't know why her every instinct insisted she should stay in her father's house come what may, but her instincts had seldom failed her in the past and she was prepared to back them now.

"Will people talk, do you think?" she asked abruptly.

"Do you care?"

Bar sat down on the chintz-covered sofa, wondering how the Allans kept their room so cool and fresh.

"The farm means a lot to me," she said slowly. "I can't go back to the life I knew in England. The house and farm are all I've got."

"Why don't you explain that to Jonathan?"

"Explain what to me?" Jonathan asked, coming into the room with Mr. Allan and smiling down at the small woman who was pouring him out a cup of tea. They were obviously very good friends, Bar decided. They had that easy air of people who don't have to explain themselves to each other. Bar couldn't remember that her parents and the Allans had ever been as sympathetic to one another as that.

"That I'm not going back to England," she said in a small voice. "And I'm not going to stay here. I prefer my own house!" She lifted her chin proudly and looked him straight in the eyes. "I'm sorry if it isn't convenient as far as you're concerned, but there's nothing else I can do."

The scar on his brow shone white against the tan of his face, making her wonder how he had come by it. It should have been disfiguring, she thought uneasily, but she found it only attractive.

"I'm sorry," she said again.

He turned away from her, helping himself to one of Mrs. Allan's cookies to go with his tea.

"If you're going to stay you'll have to work for your living," was all he said.

"I mean to. It's my farm after all."

"And I run it. If you don't or won't take my orders, you'll be out of there so fast your feet won't touch the ground." His full attention returned to her face, his eyes hard and unsympathetic. "Take it or leave it."

"I'll take it," she said.

Chapter Four

The farm office was set a little way away from the house. It had a thatched roof that creaked in the lightest wind and walls of mud and plaited wood that were pleasantly cool even in the hottest weather. Bar had always liked the office. She liked the smell of the thatch mixed with the scent of ink and paper, and she liked the work that went on there.

Not that Jonathan had done much there recently. She accepted his excuses with a pinch of salt. She had never yet met an active farmer who enjoyed doing all the necessary paperwork as well.

"I'll take over in here if you like," she offered.

His narrowed eyes took in her flushed, eager face. "Sure you want to bury yourself in office work?"

"Why not?" she countered.

"It won't earn you much male admiration buried away in here."

"Not even yours?"

He shrugged his shoulders. "I've managed so far. However hard you work at it, you'll never be necessary to the running of the farm. As long as you realise that and it amuses you to play at being farm secretary, or whatever title you want to give yourself, I've no objection."

"How about farm owner?" Bar suggested.

"What does that make me?"

"Farm manager?"

His hand brushed against the bare skin of her arm, removing a small insect which she hadn't even noticed.

"No way," he said. "Don't go getting your hopes up, Bar. I'm boss here, and that's the way it's going to stay. You'll only get hurt if you fight me, and what would you get out of it? How long will this nostalgic kick for your lost childhood last? A month? Three months? Well, there's no way I'm going to allow you to mess up the long-term running of my farm because you're going through a particular phase in your growing up. Whatever brought you here—an unfortunate romance, jealousy of your mother's remarriage—it won't last and you'll go running back to England, eager to take up your comfortable life there where you left off. If you're going to stay around here you're going to have to prove your worth. And that goes if you stay a week, or a year. Understood?"

Her temper flared. "What will you do if I go to Nairobi and get Father's solicitor to turn you out?"

"You can't do it!"

"You can't be sure of that!"

"Try it and see," he returned grimly.

"I will!"

She regretted the words as soon as they were out. She didn't want to turn him out. All she wanted was to share the farm with him. Goodness knows, there was more than enough for both of them to do and she was beginning to think they would fit well together. Jonathan was a man of action, much as her father had been, and she was more than content to run the office and check the worksheets, provided she had the chance to get out and about every now and then. She was trained for the task. More, he needed her, and she couldn't think why he was too blind, or too stubborn to see it.

"It won't do the farm any good if we fight all the time," she said at last. "We'll have to find some way of living together. Do you agree?"

He stood in front of her, his hands on his hips, and she felt threatened by his sheer masculinity. "There's only one way we'll live together and I doubt you'd agree to it."

She tried to give him back look for look, but the width of his shoulders and the way his muscles rippled in his strong arms undermined her concentration. She shrugged her shoulders helplessly.

"Why don't you try me and see?"

"There's only one way for any man and woman to share a house. Are you inviting me to try it with you?"

She felt a weakness in her knees and sat down hastily in the swivel chair behind the magnificent hardwood desk that her father had made himself, as he had made much of the wooden furniture in the house. It was his hobby when he was married to her mother, only given up with so much else after her departure.

"Don't be ridiculous!" she said with a catch in her throat.

"You could do worse," he taunted her. "There aren't many men around here and you'll soon get lonely."

"I never have been."

"Of course not, when you were in London."

"One can be very lonely in London," she started. But how could she ever begin to explain how different she felt from her mother's friends and the people she knew in London? Their concerns had been all in their own backyard, while she had scanned the papers daily for news of Africa, only to find there was nothing at all in the newspaper her mother favoured and very little in any other. Her homeland could have been on another planet.

Jonathan raised his brows in obvious disbelief. "I've always heard you're a very popular young lady in *London*," he said.

"Who from? Father?"

He shook his head. "You seldom bothered to write to your father, so what little information about you I gleaned from him was all about your early childhood. No, I gather the Allan son is one of your many admirers, much given to tearing out his hair with jealousy of all the other young men you were going with. Never a dull moment, if he's to be believed?"

"Many a dull moment," she said on a sigh. "Like Michael himself. Nice, but dull."

"We can't all rival Lothario as lovers," Jonathan said dryly.

"I'm not asking you to try," she retorted.

He sat down on the edge of the desk, his face amused. "Aren't you?"

She hoped she looked a good deal more composed than she felt. She felt as though she had set forth on calm waters and been caught up by the edge of a whirlpool that might draw her down into its vortex inexorably, no matter how hard she tried to escape.

"I have every right to be here," she maintained stubbornly.

"So you keep saying, but I'll get rid of you in the end. You'll soon tire of the life out here, just as your mother did before you."

Her fingers found the torn edge of some blotting paper and she played with it in silence for a moment.

"It's kind of you to offer to keep me amused," she said finally, "but I think your fiancée might have something to say about that. We'll just have to see if I get bored without your attentions, won't we?" She smiled up at him, determinedly sweet.

"I'll get rid of you somehow!" he vowed with a frown.

She went on smiling. "It's dangerous to throw people away, even those you despise," she told him. "Don't you know the story of how the Maasai came by death?"

"No," he admitted. It obviously worried him that she should be so much at home with their language and their legends. It destroyed his picture of her as a sophisticated Londoner who had never seen any land wilder than Wimbledon Common and would be frightened to death if she had.

Unconsciously, she assumed the pose of storyteller, remembering how she had been told the story in the days of her youth.

"The Maasai patriarch, from whom all Maa speakers are descended," she began, "was named Leeyo. He walked and talked with the great beginner of the earth, Natero Kop, and he was instructed by him that if a child of his tribe were to die, he was to cast the body away, saying, 'Man die and come back again. Moon die and remain away.' But because the first child to die hadn't been fathered by Leeyo, he held him to be of no account and so he reversed the incantation. 'Man die and remain away,' he chanted. 'Moon die and return.' What did the rights of this child matter? It was no grief to him that the child had died, so why should he fulfil his obligations as leader of the tribe?"

"So, what happened?" Jonathan interrupted her.

Bar resumed her pose. "The next child to die was one of Leeyo's own, one of his favourite children. This time he carried out the ceremony as Natero Kop had first instructed him. 'Man die and come back again. Moon die and remain away.' The child didn't return though. Natero Kop told him it was too late, he had spoilt things for his own child by the way he had treated the first one. Now all men would die and only the moon would come back to life again, month after month. If you throw away my rights to the farm, you may find you've thrown away the farm too. Think about it."

"I've managed up to now."

Bar shook her head. "It was my father's farm. He was bad enough when it came to paperwork, but have you even looked in here since he died?"

Jonathan looked absurdly guilty. "Not often," he admitted.

"Exactly." Bar pressed home her advantage dryly. "But perhaps your fiancée—?"

"You're a bit premature in calling her that, and no, she's no farmer. Few women are."

"Bigoted to the last, aren't you? My father can remember women farmers doing well out here when he was a child!"

"Maybe. I can't check with him now, can I?"

Bar bit her lip. For a minute there she had forgotten her father was dead and that she was the only Nelson left to carry on the battle for the Nelson farm.

"Didn't he ever mention them to you? One of them was German with a funny name."

"Oh yes, I met her before she died. A tough old bird, but splendid in her way. Is that what you want to turn into?"

"I could do worse."

He grinned at her. "I prefer you the way you are."

Bar could feel herself blushing. "I'm overcome!" she mocked him. "I thought you didn't like me at all?"

"It depends what for."

She felt more uncomfortable than ever under his knowing gaze. If she had had half the experience he credited her with she would know exactly what to say to throw him off balance and win the trick, she thought. As it was, every advantage seemed to be his and it wasn't fair. It was her father who had wrung the farm out of the virgin land. The farm was a part of her heritage, so why should he do everything he could to spoil things for her?

"It's settled then," she said abruptly. "I take charge in here and you go on as you did before?"

"We'll try it—for a while," he agreed.

She thought it better to settle for that than to argue with him further. She found it unsettling having him so close. She could smell the scent of him, mixed with his after-shave lotion, and it was a heady mixture. Besides, she didn't like the way he was looking at her. Wasn't one fiancée enough for him to be going on with? He had accused her of predatory ways, but she thought it very much a case of the pot calling the kettle black.

"Then if you'll clear out, I'll get started," she said aloud.

He turned his head to hide his amusement. "Aren't we going to seal the bargain with a kiss?"

She looked at him through her lashes, pretending she was studying the paper in front of her. She could see clearly the scar on his brow and the break in his nose. It gave him a dominant look, like a prizefighter posing for publicity photos. Only she had no intention of being floored by him.

"I prefer to shake hands on it," she said.

He stood up, bending down over her. "Well, I don't," he said softly, running a finger down her nose. "Yours is straight enough for both of us," he added more quietly still.

She blushed scarlet, caught entirely on the wrong foot. "How did you do it?" she asked before she had thought.

He smiled straight into her eyes. "Proving my manhood."

If he could guess what was going through her mind, she had no entrance into his. It was a closed book to her. She puzzled over it for a moment. The Maasai used to prove their manhood by killing a lion single-handed, but he could hardly have meant anything like that, or could he?

She lowered her eyes. "She must've been very angry with you," she said in dulcet tones.

"A veritable virago!"

"Serves you right!"

His lips touched hers and the shock of it passed right through her body. "Mmm, nice," he said. His mouth took possession of hers, his hand on the back of her head keeping her where he wanted her. She was afraid her hair would come down under such treatment and she tried to back away from him. The pressure of his mouth increased, demanding entrance, and, when she tasted his tongue against hers, she forgot all about her hair, forgot everything but the pleasure of the sensation he was arousing in her. Her arms went up round his neck and she wound her body closer against his, enjoying the hardness of his muscles against the softer curves of hers.

He lifted her clear out of the chair and pulled the pins out of her hair, throwing them with abandon on the floor. Her hair swung down over her shoulders, a lock of fair hair clinging to his shirt.

"You look less like a London woman now!" he said.

She caught her breath. "What does a London woman look like?"

"Smooth and cool, with never a hair out of place."

"No wonder I never took to city life," she whispered against his lips.

He straightened his back, smiling down at her as he deliberately undid the top button of her blouse.

"The call of the wild gets to us all from time to time," he mocked her.

She touched his nose with one finger. "It got to you with a vengeance," she retorted. "Perhaps you should be more careful in future?"

"It's you who should be careful." There was a hint of menace in his voice that made her spine tingle. "You're too cool to be true. It'd be quite a challenge to light your fires, Miss Nelson, and find out what kind of woman you really are."

She put her hands against his chest and pushed away from him. "You make things too complicated," she complained. "I'm the simple kind, like my father. All I want is my own, and you belong to someone else! Let me go and get out of here, or I'll call Solomon to put you out!"

"Will you though?"

She opened her mouth to call Solomon's name, but it didn't work out as she'd intended. His lips closed over hers, stilling the sound, his hands travelling down her back to her hips, holding her close against him.

She tore herself free. It was one of the hardest things she had ever done. She liked the feel of his hard strength against her increasing weakness.

"Get out!" she begged.

He was surprisingly gentle with her. He helped her back into the swivel chair, retaining her hands in both his.

"Not quite so experienced as you pretend?" he murmured kindly.

"I don't pretend anything!"

"And I thought you such a cool lady. . . ."

Her eyes stung. "So I am! If I seem upset, it's

because I'm not accustomed to being mauled against my will."

His eyebrows lifted, but he said nothing. He let go of her hands slowly, allowing her fingers to slide through his as if she was as reluctant to lose contact as he.

"I'll leave you to it," he said. "I'll get Solomon to bring you over a cup of tea. All right?"

She nodded her head, unable to speak at all, at least not without making a fool of herself. It would have been the last straw to have burst into tears while he was still there, watching it all and feeling nothing. Hadn't he got a perfectly good woman of his own? Mrs. Allan had certainly told her so. That succeeded in arousing her anger and she felt distinctly better. How dare he carry on with her behind the other girl's back?

"If it happens again I'll tell your fiancée!" she warned him.

His eyes narrowed a little as he looked at her. "Is that a challenge?"

She sniffed. "Perhaps I won't bother. You're just the sort of person who'd have an agreement for each of you to go your own ways. You haven't any real feelings for anyone!"

"Particularly not for you," he agreed cheerfully.

"I know that!"

"Well, of course not! You're the one I want to get rid of, remember? Don't you wish you were safely in England now?"

She did not! She wanted to be exactly where she was, a thought not likely to add to her sense of comfort. She shouldn't want to skirmish with Jonathan! She shouldn't want to have anything to do with him! But the fact that she did was something she could feel in every cell in her body. She gave him a swift, oblique look.

"I must go and feed the gazelle," she muttered. "Get out of my way!"

He grinned at her, the lines caused by squinting into a hot sun deepening round his eyes and from nose to mouth.

"I seldom take orders from anyone," he told her.

"Not even my father?"

"We didn't have that sort of relationship."

"Well, you do with me!"

His smile faded. "I shouldn't be too sure of that," he said.

She pushed past him, not daring to linger any longer in that close, intimate atmosphere. Outside, she took several deep breaths, filling her lungs with the hot, sun-filled air of Africa. She wasn't going to allow Jonathan to spoil any of this for her, she vowed. Not now, not *ever!*

The fawn was stirring in his makeshift bed when she entered the kitchen. Solomon was busy at the stove, doing she knew not what. In her experience, all Africans had a strange approach to cooking, often beginning with the last course and working backwards, putting dishes in and out of the oven whenever it moved them to do so, sometimes taking the whole day to cook a simple joint of meat. The results, however, were almost invariably splendid. She had sometimes wondered if most things weren't all the better for being rested at intervals in their cooking. She remembered saying as much to her mother only to receive a very sharp answer. Her mother believed her ways were the right ways and all other ways were slovenly or worse.

Bar picked up the gazelle and cuddled it closely against her body. She noted her hands were trembling after her encounter with Jonathan and wondered at her lack of control.

"The milk is ready," Solomon told her without turning round.

"I wonder if the mixture is rich enough," Bar worried to herself.

"Goat milk would be better."

Solomon had lived in Maasai country almost all his adult life, but he had never forgotten that his own tribe tilled the land and kept sheep and goats rather than cattle. In his own way, he looked down on the tall, stringy, ultra-proud Maasai, quite as much as they looked down on him.

"We'd have to buy the goat first," Bar dismissed the idea.

Solomon shook his head. "My wife keeps goats for the children. She can spare you a little milk. Shall I fetch you some?"

Bar thanked him. She was glad to have a little time alone with the gazelle, to pet it and make friends with it. She was glad to see how well it was doing now it had got used to its new surroundings. She even thought it looked a little fatter than it had the day before.

"Aren't you going to sing to it today?" Jonathan asked her from the doorway.

"I might."

"Don't let me stop you," he said ironically.

She bent her head over the gazelle. "I'm not a

fool," she rounded on him, "and one would have to be a fool not to know why you resent my singing in Maa!"

"Because I can't speak Maa myself?"

"Exactly."

"You would think that," he said, almost complacently. "I comfort myself with the knowledge that I can do other things better than you can."

She rose to the bait, whirling round to face him. "What can you do better?"

Her hair was all over the place and he came over to her, pushing it back over her shoulders. "Who was it who got the fawn to take its milk?" he mocked her. He chucked the small animal under the chin, smiling down at it as it accepted his tickling finger with soporific enjoyment.

"After I'd done all the softening-up process," she claimed, not knowing if it were true or not.

"Is that what you're doing to me?"

She stared at him. "Of course not!"

"It might work," he went on. "But you'd have realised that. Isn't that how your mother has always got her own way, by using her charms on any male who can give it to her?"

Bar winced. "You've never met my mother—" she began angrily.

"No, but I've met you."

She offered no objection at all when he took the fawn from her and put it back in its box. There was no strength left in her limbs to do more than stand and wait. She felt confused and a little frightened.

"You've been biased against me from the start. You may be right that I should have joined my father earlier. I wanted to, but it seemed best to finish at college first. It's easy to say that my qualifications don't matter much compared with missing seeing him again, but I didn't know that then."

His jaw tightened, a muscle jerking in his cheek. "None of us knew. You could have written, however."

"How d'you know I didn't?"

"Because whenever he got a letter from you—which wasn't often—he'd read it out to anyone who'd listen to him. You wrote to him as you would have done to a stranger! Your mother was well. You'd attended this dance, or that party, and you'd worn such-and-such dress. You never once mentioned coming out to see him!"

Bar blinked hastily. "But he knew—"

"He got letters from your mother too," Jonathan said dryly.

Bar could imagine what they had contained too. Her mother had never believed for an instant that Bar would actually turn her back on England and return to her father and the Africa she loved. How badly her father must have been hurt between the two of them! Her eyes misted over and she wound her long hair round her fingers, striving in vain to restore it to its usual neat French pleat.

"We left the pins in the office," Jonathan said without looking at her.

"I'll go and get them," she said on a sob. "Will you feed the fawn please?"

She rushed out of the kitchen, dodging round Solomon as he came back with the goat's milk. She had to get out of here! She had to go somewhere, anywhere, that was away from Jonathan. She scrabbled on the floor of the office, looking for the long pins with which she fastened her hair. She wouldn't work at all today, she decided fiercely. She would go over and visit the Allans and she wouldn't come back until after dark. By that time she would be herself again.

Chapter Five

"My dear child, what have you been doing with yourself?"

Bar put a self-conscious hand up to her hair, which was in acute danger of coming down again. "I lost some of my hairpins. Do I look awful?"

Mrs. Allan was a second or two making up her mind. "If you don't mind my saying so, my dear, it makes you look more human than you usually do. You have a very cool exterior—like your mother."

Bar looked straight ahead of her. "Hidden fires," she murmured. Her mother, though, was a very cool lady through and through. Bar thought she was different, but was she?

Mrs. Allan looked curious. "How did you come to lose your hairpins?" she enquired.

"They—they fell out," Bar tried to explain.

"Did they though?" her hostess said skeptically.

"By the way, Jonathan's young lady is staying with us—rather unexpectedly as far as we are concerned. Come inside and I'll introduce you to her."

Bar was glad of her ability to look cool, calm, and collected as she followed Mrs. Allan into the house. She was not looking forward to this meeting. She didn't want to know anything about Jonathan's girl friend. She kept telling herself that it was nothing to her if he had half-a-dozen lady friends, but it wasn't true. For some reason she minded very much indeed. She seized on the first logical explanation that occurred to her; it would increase the awkwardness between them of sharing the farm and, worse still, the house. Two women in the house would lead to friction, especially if they both expected to act as mistress of the place. Bar kept telling herself that her claims came first, but Jonathan had lived there for a long time now, and as an adult, not as a child.

"Does Jonathan know she's here?" she asked as they gained the cool, darkened hall.

"Do you think I should have told him?" Mrs. Allan worried.

"I don't know," Bar admitted. "Does she always stay with you?"

"She has stayed with us before," Mrs. Allan said cautiously. "A rather demanding guest, but the least said about that the better. We're not used to receiving the cream of society out here and I think I must have lost the knack of doing things with the same flair they have in Nairobi. I feel very much the country cousin!"

Bar laughed. "I think you're lovely! You don't know what a relief it is to come and go as one likes, without having to dress up all the time."

"Clothes always meant a lot to your mother," Mrs. Allan agreed. "She had an advantage on the rest of us of being able to look like a fashion plate in an old sack. She was right in a way, you know. It's all too easy to let oneself go and not bother about how one looks for months together. It's very bad for the morale!"

If that was true, the young woman who was seated on the chintz-covered sofa in the sitting room was in no danger of losing her confidence. She was about the most beautiful person Bar had ever seen. Her hair was bleached to a silver blond, and her eyes were the next best thing to the violets that grew in the English hedgerows. She was dressed in a tailored cream skirt with a matching shirt and a black, knotted tie. She wouldn't have been overdressed at the average cocktail party.

"Felice, this is our near neighbour, Bar Nelson. Bar, our houseguest, Mrs. Felice Arghetti."

"*Mrs*. Arghetti," Bar repeated.

"I'm getting a divorce." Felice's eyes were hard and dangerous. "I heard you were here. It's why I came as a matter of fact. It sounded as though Jonathan needed someone to look after him."

Bar opened her eyes wide. "Jonathan?"

"Aren't you trying to take his farm away from him?"

"The farm is half mine, maybe even more mine than that. It started out being my father's farm, you know."

"So what? It was pretty rundown when Jonathan came along. Your father may have been the nominal owner, but it's Jonathan's work that's made the place what it is. Mr. Nelson had gone to pieces long before."

"He had a nervous breakdown," Mrs. Allan interposed gently. "He made a complete recovery, however. He and Jonathan worked very well together."

Felice turned her full gaze onto Bar. "Which is how you plan to take over?" she suggested.

"I plan to live here," Bar said.

"Not if I have anything to do with it, you won't. Jonathan will have to buy you out. That shouldn't be too hard to manage!"

"Except that I won't sell."

"Don't be ridiculous! You couldn't run the farm on your own!"

"I could, you know," Bar said casually. "What's more, I'm trained to cope with the paperwork too. Jonathan and my father were both ostriches where government forms are concerned, convinced that if they stuck their heads in the sand for long enough they'd go away in a puff of smoke. Jonathan needs me as much, if not more, than I need him."

Felice turned away, shrugging her shoulders. "He can pay a farm secretary surely. I could do it on my head. I do have secretarial experience, though of course I'm in management now."

"What do you do?" Bar asked her.

Felice was astonished that she didn't know. She caught herself up with a start and half-laughed. "My husband, Luciano, is working for the French space project down at the coast. They're building a telescope there. I run the office in Nairobi. I'm useful to them there since I speak French and Italian, as well as English."

"I see," said Bar without much interest.

"Luciano wanted me to live in Malindi with him, but I hate that sticky heat. We seldom see each other nowadays." Felice stroked her bare arms with her beautifully manicured hands and laughed softly. "Nairobi has always been my home. Jonathan doesn't know how flattered he should be that I'm considering leaving all my friends and interests there —for him."

"I prefer it here," Bar said stubbornly. "I like the open space."

"Nairobi has that too! What other city has a wild-life park in its suburbs?"

"Oh quite," said Bar. "But it's rather overcivilised compared with this!"

"One can see the animals in comfort!" Felice retorted dryly.

"It's better than nothing," Bar agreed. "But some of the animals have to be hand-fed now. Wild animals are too grand to be caged, even in a park. They ought to be free to go where they will."

"Pity your father didn't think that," Felice sniffed. "I was scared silly by that lion of his."

"He should have trained it to go free—"

Felice shuddered. "It would always have been coming back for food. Jonathan says there are few lazier creatures than lions."

Not for the first time since meeting Felice, Bar wished she had taken the trouble to wash and change before dashing over to the Allans. She felt a mess, with her hair hanging down, and she was sure her lips were bruised from Jonathan's kiss.

"Round here one can come across lions any

time," she volunteered. "I saw a pride sleeping in the sun yesterday."

"Weren't you frightened?"

Bar shook her head. "One's quite safe as long as one stays in one's vehicle. They've got used to the smell of cars and petrol fumes and hardly bother to move out of their way."

Felice was unimpressed. "When I marry Jonathan, I'm going to have a fence built round the house to keep out all the animals and the savages."

Mrs. Allan took in the look on Bar's face and hastily offered both her guests tea. "I'll just go and make it," she added.

"As long as it's something recognisable," Felice told her grandly. "I don't drink just anything labelled tea. I prefer Earl Grey—"

"I only have Kenya teas."

Felice shrugged elegant shoulders. "Then it'll have to do, won't it? Some people think Kenya teas are all right actually, but the imported ones do have that extra something, don't they?"

"Yes, price," Bar said succinctly.

Mrs. Allan definitely fluttered, which was so unlike her that Bar offered to go and make the tea for her. "Would you, dear? Kalau will show you where we keep the best tea."

To Bar's amusement, the African who did most of the cooking in the Allan household knew of only one brand of tea in the cupboard. He scratched his head under his chef's hat and clicked his tongue in anguish.

"The memsahib always uses the same tea," he told her in Swahili.

"Then we'll use that," Bar decided.

Bar found it difficult to imagine that Felice could find anything wrong with Kenya tea. Even Bar's mother prized it as highly as the most expensive brands that could be bought in London. Kenya coffee was perhaps the more famous product, but Kenya tea was fragrant and full of body.

Someone came into the house, whistling. Bar paused in measuring out the tea to listen more closely. Whoever it was could whistle as well as anyone she had ever heard. It couldn't be Mr. Allan because she knew that he didn't know one note from another and never had. She stuck her head out of the kitchen just in time to see Jonathan's back disappearing into the sitting room. What was he feeling so cheerful about? she wondered.

She added another cup to the tray, made sure the water was boiling before Kalau poured it over the leaves, and then carried the tray through the hall to the sitting room. Jonathan relieved her of it as soon as he saw her.

"Smells good," he said appreciatively.

Bar cast a look of triumph in Felice's direction, but the other girl looked as smug as a cat seated on a forbidden cushion.

"It's only tea," Bar said.

He smiled directly at her. "But look who made it!"

"Kalau did," Bar said lightly, seating herself as far away from Felice as she could.

Only Mrs. Allan laughed. Felice had a sulky mouth in repose, Bar thought. She would have to be careful if she didn't want to get some hard lines between her mouth and chin. The thought gave her pleasure and she dwelt on it for a long moment without listening to what Felice was saying.

When she did start to listen, it was some time before she realised she was talking about her father's house.

"It isn't livable in as it is. *You* may have found it so, living as two bachelors there together and out most of the time, but I'm accustomed to better things! In my apartment in Nairobi I have every conceivable convenience to hand."

Bar started to laugh. "We're not short of gadgets, the only trouble is when *someone* forgets to start up the generator and there's no electricity."

"Do you want to take over the job?" Jonathan asked her.

Bar met the challenge head on. "Why not?"

"Okay. Try it, and see how you get on. It'll be my turn to complain when the lights fail!"

Felice looked thoroughly annoyed. "Wouldn't it be better if one of you moved out?" she demanded. "It isn't right for you to be there together. I'm sure Alice—"

"Alice?" Bar said blankly.

"Alice is my name," Mrs. Allan told her with a smile. "You were too young to use it when you were here before and your mother didn't approve of the prefix of aunt unless there was a real relationship. Please call me Alice now."

"Thank you," Bar managed, knowing that Mrs. Allan would always be Mrs. Allan to her.

"Alice and Peter would be glad to have you," Felice went on with more determination than she had showed about anything else. "If there isn't room for us both, I'll go back with Jonathan."

Mrs. Allan looked suddenly more cheerful. "We'd be very glad to have you, Bar. We offered before—"

"I know. Don't think I don't appreciate the offer, but I prefer to live in my own house. Why don't you have Jonathan stay with you?"

Mrs. Allan cast her a reproachful look. "It might be better if Felice stayed with you," she suggested hopefully. "You have the room, don't you?"

Bar's eyelashes swept up, giving a mischievous slant to her face. "Complete with a large variety of insects! The oil lamps seem to attract them even more than electricity does."

"Don't you flit your rooms?" Felice asked with naked distaste.

"It doesn't seem to make much difference, what with my comings and goings to feed my baby gazelle every two hours. The house seemed full of nocturnal creatures by the time I'd finished."

Jonathan was amused. "I guess they liked your Maa nursery songs better than I did!"

Felice's face was a study. "Do you speak Maa?" she asked Bar in tones of horror.

"Don't you?" Bar riposted.

"I speak a little kitchen Swahili—one has to after all, but to actually learn to speak the local languages! Well, it's rather an eccentric thing to do, isn't it? I mean who would there be to talk to when one had mastered it?"

Bar wondered why Felice should choose to live in Africa. A strong desire to be rude almost overcame her, but she restrained herself just in time, making a joke of it instead.

"I talk to my gazelle," she said.

Jonathan glanced up. "Did you retain your Kenyan nationality?" he asked suddenly.

Bar nodded. "Of course."

"I shouldn't have thought you'd have wanted to. I don't suppose your mother did?"

"My mother never had Kenyan citizenship."

"But you have?"

Bar gave him look for look. "It was a conscious choice," she told him. "I knew I'd come home sooner or later."

"Home?" Felice repeated. "Your home is in England! The sooner you return there the better! Jonathan agrees with me that you'll never settle down out here. It's a rotten life for any woman, as your mother, and I for that matter, could tell you!"

"Then why do you stay?" Bar countered, disliking Felice more by the minute.

Felice looked demure. "Because of Jonathan, why else? Besides, I've always lived here. It makes a difference."

"Your husband works in this country," Jonathan added, drawling out the words. "Didn't that have something to do with it?"

Felice smiled at him. "Well, of course, it did, but I try not to think about that these days. It's no good making oneself miserable over nothing, is it?" She turned her attention back to the problem of the Nelson house. "If there really are as many insects as Barbara makes out in your house at night, why don't you net all the windows? I could take the measurements and have the screens made up for you in Nairobi?" She shivered delicately. "I couldn't share any house of mine with the night life you get around here."

"Nobody's asking you to!" Bar flashed out. Then she wished the words unsaid. She wondered why Jonathan wanted to tie himself up with a woman who obviously had no feeling for his chosen way of life. From a man's point of view, Felice obviously had other qualities, most of them unpleasant to Bar's way of thinking, but it was really no business of hers.

Felice's mouth quivered, but her eyes remained as hard as sapphires. "Somebody has to make the house bearable," she snapped. "Neither Jonathan nor you show any sign of doing so! You're both totally uncivilised."

Bar's anger boiled within her, but Jonathan was amused.

"You're quite right, my dear," he said mildly.

"It's nothing to be proud of!" Felice told him.

"On the contrary, I was admiring your perspicacity in seeing through Bar's London gloss at a glance." He looked critically at the furious Bar. "Though, come to think of it," he went on, "she's not looking her usual immaculate self."

Bar glared at him, daring him to make anything more of their exchange earlier that morning. Her fury simmered as his amused, knowing eyes met hers.

"Did something upset you?" he taunted her.

"Certainly not!"

"My mistake. I thought something must have happened to have made you lose your cool."

She was tempted to say that meeting Felice Arghetti had been quite enough to put her in a bad humour but she didn't have a chance because Felice was talking again.

"I don't care how you want to live, Jonathan, but

I'm warning you, you won't get me to live in that house without a great many changes made. I'll drive over later and draw up a list—"

"No, you won't!" Bar told her.

"I won't what?" A pained puzzlement crossed Felice's near-perfect features.

"You won't step foot in my house until you're invited by me!"

Felice stood up, her fists clenched. "How dare you speak to me like that?" she demanded. "You know nothing about anything! You may think you do because you can remember a little of some obscure African language from your childhood, but you don't! What do you know of life out here, with your English ways and your London clothes?"

Bar glanced meaningly down at her own "off-the-peg" shirt and slacks and then at Felice's beautifully tailored skirt.

"I can tell you one thing," she said, her voice lazy and indifferent, which was something she thought she had learned in England. Never show your feelings in public, her mother had warned her again and again, when Bar had been bored at a party, or by the particular young man her parent had selected to escort her.

"Yes?"

Bar made herself smile. "Africa has a way of exacting a terrible revenge from those who live off her but don't love her."

"I've lived here all my life! I don't need teaching about this country from you!"

Bar gave her a look of pure scorn. "You don't know the land at all!" she said.

Jonathan rose to his feet also, giving Felice a

perfunctory kiss on the cheek before she could say anything more.

"I think it's time I took our African firebrand home," he said to Mrs. Allan. "She'll be taking us all on if we don't look out."

Alice Allan shot a quick look at Felice and back to Jonathan. "Bar's right—in a way. When she was a baby she was practically raised by the Maasai. She knows things that those of us who came here as adults can never know. I thought she might have lost that, living in England with her mother all these years, but—"

"What can she possibly know that's of any use to people like us?" Felice asked with a curl of the lip. "Speaking for myself, I don't think there's anything I can learn from the Maasai. They live on a revolting diet and have diseased cattle that would be better off put down. What else does one need to know about them?"

Bar set her chin at a belligerent angle. "They know how to live with the land and to get the best out of it."

"With their methods of farming?"

"The Maasai don't farm. They're a pastoral people. Nor would the land support much more than their cattle and the wild animals who've always lived on it. How many white farmers do you know who ploughed up the land and lived to regret it in erosion and crop failures?"

"Quite a few," Jonathan unexpectedly agreed with her.

"Your father didn't do much better!" Felice said nastily.

"He never put more into the land than he took out

of it," his erstwhile partner defended him. "He had some very interesting ideas of farming the indigenous animals when I first joined him. But he lost heart when his wife left him. He might have done better to have followed her back to England."

Bar held her breath, saddened by this confirmation of how badly her father had taken her mother's desertion. "It wasn't a bad idea though, was it?" she appealed to Jonathan. "Do you think we might try it again?"

"You're not going to try anything on Jonathan's farm!" Felice answered for him. "What do you know about it anyway?"

Jonathan raised his eyebrows and his scar showed very white. "She has book learning. There'll be no holding her if she ever gets some practical experience as well!"

Felice came forward and put a possessive hand on his arm, brushing her fingers through the coating of hair that covered his forearms.

"You're not going to let her learn her trade on your farm, are you?" she murmured.

"I may not have any choice, seeing that Nelson left her his share in the property."

"You can get the will overturned!"

"I can try," he agreed cheerfully. "Just as soon as I get the time to consult a lawyer about it. Are you coming, Bar?"

Bar longed to tell him what he could do with his lawyer. If she wasn't entitled to her father's interest in the farm, who was? What was he waiting for, anyway? She was sure Felice would oblige by consulting the lawyer on his behalf. His fiancée was even more eager to get rid of Bar than was Jonathan.

Felice's hold on his arm tightened. She had grasp-
ing hands, Bar thought, gazing distastefully at the
painted nails. The hands of a taker who had very
little to give in return.

"Darling, I haven't any transport with me. Can I
borrow your Landrover while I'm here?"

Jonathan's jaw tightened. It was a look Bar was
getting to know very well and she waited for him to
refuse, as she knew he would have refused her.

"Where do you want to go?" he asked.

Felice spread her fingers. "About." She peeked up
at him through her lashes. "I may come visiting you.
That's why I flew down here. Please, Jonathan!"

Jonathan's face softened. "I'll cadge a lift home
with my reluctant partner. Come on, Bar, let's go."

Bar swallowed a disbelieving lump in her throat.
"I don't want you coming with me!" she protested.

She searched in her handbag for the keys, shocked
by a trembling sensation in her middle that told her
she did want him to go with her, very badly, not that
it meant she was going to say so.

"You don't have any choice!" he told her.

He waited with ill-concealed impatience while she
said goodbye to Mrs. Allan and the older woman
begged her to come over as often as she could. The
two women exchanged conspiratorial grins and Bar
knew Jonathan had seen the exchange and that he
must have gathered that neither of them cared for
his near-fiancée.

Bar walked out to her own vehicle, ignoring
Felice's limp, belatedly offered hand, torn away
from Jonathan's arm with difficulty. She got into the
driving seat and blew the horn.

"I thought you were in a hurry!" she said to

Jonathan, after she had watched with interest as he received a loving goodbye kiss and a whispered message from Felice.

He came across to her truck, his lips pressed together in tight disapproval. "Move over!" he commanded her. "I'll drive!"

"Not my car, you won't!"

He gave her a weary look. "Stop playing games, Bar. Hand over the keys and move over."

She sat where she was, glowering at him. When he made no move, she reached over and opened the passenger door for him. It was a mistake. He opened her own door and lifted her bodily into the passenger seat, sitting down in the driving seat himself and turning on the ignition key.

They drove in silence for a mile or two, then Bar said, "Wouldn't it be better if Felice broke off with her old husband before she took on a new one?"

"What has it got to do with you?" Jonathan grunted.

"Plenty, seeing it's my house she wants to alter."

"We've yet to see whose house it is. Felice has had an unhappy couple of years. Why don't you try a more friendly approach with her?"

"She's not living in my house! The two of you will have to build one of your own, preferably out of sight of mine!"

"You may get married yourself," he reminded her, relaxing visibly.

"I've no plans for doing so. You have!"

He shook his head at her, slowing to a stop by the side of the road. "What a nice gossip you must have had before I came along. You shouldn't believe all you hear, or all that you read in wills!"

She turned to face him, to tell him once and for all that she was never, *never* going to give up her inheritance. To her surprise he was smiling. Her mouth felt suddenly dry and there was a tingling sensation in her spine.

"Can't we work something out?" she asked him.

He leaned over and planted a kiss full on her half-open mouth. Her arms closed round his neck and he kissed her again, before pushing her away from him.

"We'll talk about it sometime," he said.

Chapter Six

Bar looked round the office with a feeling of satisfaction. Where chaos had reigned, now everything was neat and tidy. Forms had been filled in, letters sent off, records kept up to date, and she could now lay her hands on the relevant items that dealt with every aspect of the farm's management. To achieve this, she had worked around the clock for a week. Of Jonathan she had seen nothing at all, still less of Felice. Once or twice she had heard a female voice in the house, but she had always stepped across to the office before she could be put in the position of having to act as hostess to someone she disliked.

She was surprised when Jonathan came into the office to find her with time on her hands for the first time since she had taken it over.

"Nothing to do?" he accused her.

"Nothing at the moment," she replied guardedly, wondering what was coming next.

He opened and shut one or two of the files, riffling through her neat documentation. "You've done a good job," he commented. "Fell like a change of pace?"

"It depends."

His expression was bland. "You could do with a day off. You know the saying, all work and no play makes Jill a dull girl? You can ride a horse, can't you? Come out and see what we're doing outside."

Bar pursed her lips thoughtfully. "What about Felice? Or do you mean for her to come too?"

"She doesn't ride."

Bar opened her eyes wide. "No?" she marvelled. "What is she going to do with herself when she comes to live here?"

"Let's leave Felice out of this! D'you want to come or not? We have to make arrangements for dipping the cattle sometime soon and I want to discuss it with the Maasai. You could be useful there."

Bar sat back in her chair. "And Felice wouldn't be?"

"She's always decorative. That's an asset in any woman," he retorted.

"From whose point of view?"

"Even the Maasai must prefer a pretty woman to a plain one."

Bar fell silent. Was she so plain? She had studied her appearance long and hard in the looking glass after returning from the Allans the week before and she hadn't come up with many answers. Felice's doll-like features had left her dissatisfied with her own smiling mouth and tip-tilted nose, just as the other girl's perfectly bleached hair had made her own look and feel mousy and ordinary.

"Maasai women work for their living," she said.

"Do you think Felice doesn't?"

"Does she?"

Jonathan looked down his nose at her. "She might not have got the job if it hadn't been for Luciano, but I imagine she functions quite satisfactorily or they wouldn't have kept her on." His lips twitched. "She does speak both French and Italian very well."

"Civilised languages!" Bar said in disgust. "What have we come to when citizens of this country don't even speak the language of their fellow citizens?"

"There are so many of them," Jonathan pointed out.

"*Everyone* speaks Swahili!"

"So does Felice."

"Kitchen Swahili. Do this, do that, cook things you've never heard of and wouldn't dream of eating yourself, and never, never expect me to treat you like a person at all."

Jonathan touched her cheek with the fingers of one hand, drawing them across her mouth and running his forefinger around her lips.

"You shouldn't make such harsh judgements about someone you've made no effort to get to know," he rebuked her.

"I know her well enough!" Bar protested.

Jonathan shook his head. "You forget how long you've been away. You still see this country through the eyes of a twelve-year-old and make your judge-

ments accordingly. Why don't you look about you
and see what's happening here now? You may even
understand people like Felice better."

"And how about people like you?" If he thought
he could persuade her to look on him in a more
kindly light, he would hope in vain. All he wanted
was to be rid of her, but there was no way that she
would be leaving.

He actually smiled. "I don't think you see me
through the eyes of a twelve-year-old—not all the
time," he mocked her.

She was immediately indignant. "Just because I've
let you kiss me once or twice, don't go building up
your hopes about—" She broke off, not knowing
how to finish the sentence. As far as she knew, he
hadn't built up his hopes about anything as far as she
was concerned.

"You forget, I have Felice to keep me happy," he
drawled. "How about you?"

"I'm happy as I am!" She was silent for a minute,
her dislike of Felice so vivid that she could taste it on
her tongue.

"You look it!" he mocked her.

"Oh, let's go!" she said. "It always takes a long
time to persuade the Maasai that if we help dip their
cattle it's only fair they help dip ours."

Jonathan looked thoughtfully at her. "We haven't
allowed them to dip their beasts with ours in recent
years."

Bar gaped at him. "Why ever not? I suppose that
was your idea to save money? Well, let me tell you
it's a false economy! My father always said so,
because the cattle are always getting mixed up, and

anyway we run them quite close enough for them to pick up every disease that's going from each other."

"He changed his mind later on."

"You must have changed it for him!"

"No, that was his side of the business. We had a lot of losses because the young warriors had nothing better to do than knock off our cattle with their bows and arrows."

"More likely with their spears," Bar interrupted him.

"However it was, it couldn't go on, so Bob stopped them dipping their cattle."

"He must have been mad!" Bar exclaimed.

"He was," Jonathan agreed grimly.

Bar chewed on her lower lip. "I think I'd better discuss it with the elders before we do anything else," she said at last. "It's too far to go by horse. Shall we go in your car or mine?"

"Felice has mine," he reminded her somewhat sourly.

Bar grinned. "So she has! You can't come with me unless you allow me to drive. I'd sooner go by myself."

Jonathan's eyes swept over her. "Right, you do that. I'll take the day off and go over to the Allans and help entertain Felice. She wouldn't fancy a day out with the Maasai."

"No, she wouldn't," Bar agreed with a promptness she knew would annoy him. "I can see you're going to be very well matched!"

"I'm glad you think so."

He was gone soon after that, leaving Bar to reflect that somewhere along the line she seemed to have lost her touch when it came to dealing with men. In all their clashes Jonathan always managed to get the last word and she was left feeling both foolish and bereft. If she had played her cards better, she thought, she would have been the one to have Jonathan's company all day. Instead, she had succeeded in handing him over to Felice on a plate and the other girl would make the most of it, of that she was sure.

With his going, the office had lost much of its appeal for her. What had Felice been doing while she was slaving away, avoiding Jonathan as much as she had Felice? It wouldn't have been so bad if he had been pleased by the results, bowled over by her efficiency, but it was obviously far more important to him how a woman looked. Did Felice find his brand of kisses as devastating as she did? She could only presume she did.

It was hot in the Landcruiser. The seat burned her through the thin material of her trousers and the engine got so hot that the pedals felt like fire beneath her feet. To add to her troubles, Tikipit's family had moved since her last visit to his mother. She came across the empty encampment and was astonished by how tatty and neglected it looked in a couple of days. True, the enclosure had been broken down and the abandoned huts inside had been broken open, so that in a week or two it would be impossible to tell that anyone had ever lived on that particular spot.

Bar sighed to herself. She could spend the whole day looking for their new encampment and she might not find it yet. She drove up to the summit of a small hill in the middle of the plain and trained her field glasses onto the waving, golden grass, hoping she might see a puff of giveaway smoke somewhere in the distance. There was nothing to be seen.

Perhaps, she thought, she had lost the art of sensing the movements of other living creatures about her. As a child, she could have tracked an animal for miles, following its tracks as easily as Tikipit would. Now she felt as helpless as she had when first faced with a modern city, skyscrapers and paved streets. Getting round London had frightened her far more than the wild animals had back in Africa. Was it now going to be the other way round?

Something moved just ahead of her and she saw the tall, spare figure of a Maasai *moran* walking towards her. Content, she sat back in her seat and waited for him to come up to her.

"Jambo. Habari?" she greeted him.

He froze, as still as any statue, then came more slowly towards her.

"Mzuri," he answered reluctantly.

Bar switched to his own tongue, asking him where she would find the dwelling of Tikipit's family. He pointed across the plain with his spear and came a little closer, smiling to reveal beautifully spaced, very white teeth.

"Tikipit is a married man at last. Will you visit with his wife?"

"And his mother."

The young warrior thought about this. "'Tis well," he approved finally. "I have more important matters on my mind."

"Not my cattle, I hope?" Bar enquired gently.

His grin widened. "A man should kill a lion, not the pet of a woman."

Bar smiled also. "The lions are protected by the government," she reminded him. "My cattle are not."

"This lion must be killed. She is not afraid of people. If I don't kill her, she'll kill our children, but first I have to find her. When I've slain her, the women will sing songs about me for many years to come!"

Bar started up the engine of the Landcruiser. "I hope you have a licence from the government," she said by way of a parting shot.

"The government is far away, the lion is here."

That would be the answer, if not for always, at least for a long time to come, Bar thought as she drove across the plains in the direction the *moran* had pointed out to her. The Maasai lived by their own laws now, just as they had in British times and before, and they wouldn't change easily.

Tikipit did her the honour of coming out of his compound to greet her. He carried a staff instead of a spear now that he was a married elder, and he leaned against it, placing one foot on the thigh of his other leg in an attitude all Maasai men learn as children.

"My wife will be overcome that you should visit her. She is building us a new shelter, but my mother thinks poorly of her efforts."

What mother-in-law did not? Bar leaned back against the bonnet of the Landcruiser and yelped with pain. When she had sufficiently recovered herself, she opened the door and sat down on the driving seat instead.

"I came to see you as well as your wife," she told

Tikipit. "It's the time of year for dipping the cattle. Will you bring yours to be done as you used to do?"

"I will ask the other elders what they think. Your father hasn't allowed us to bring our cattle anywhere near his these last years."

"My father is dead."

"What does your man say? This is no matter for a woman to decide."

Bar cursed all men under her breath. Did they all think that no woman could do anything on her own account?

"He sent me to speak for him," she compromised aloud, despising herself as she did so.

"Tell him I'll bring him his answer in the morning," Tikipit said firmly.

"He doesn't speak Maa," Bar couldn't resist saying.

"But his Swahili is better than yours," Tikipit told her. "He is welcome amongst us."

Bar was impressed, knowing that the Maasai thought all other men inferior to themselves. "I'll tell Jonathan what you say," she said.

She took the long way home, lonely after her visit as she had not expected to be. She couldn't forget that Jonathan was with Felice. As she drove home the long way round, she tried to put him out of her mind. It should have been an easy thing to do, but even though she could briefly control her thoughts, her body remembered exactly how she had felt when he touched her. Her heart ached with the memory and her stomach felt like a nest of butterflies. Well, he would not be thinking about her, she surmised. He would have his hands full with Felice Arghetti.

When she hesitated at a place where two tracks met, the smell of lion came at her through the open window. She looked about, wondering if they would still be close by, but there was nothing to be seen, only a few zebra searching for something to eat beneath a clump of fever trees.

Jonathan was home before her. She could tell he was in a bad temper the moment she set eyes on him and for some reason her own spirits rose accordingly.

"How did you get on?" he called out to her from the verandah. He had a glass of beer in his hand and he looked as though he would like to have poured it all over her.

"Tikipit'll bring the answer in the morning."

Jonathan raised a smile. "So, they wouldn't talk to you after all?"

But Bar refused to admit as much. "Naturally they wanted to discuss it between themselves first."

"Naturally," he said dryly.

She smiled sunnily at him. "How did your day go?"

He didn't answer immediately. "Have a beer?" he said instead.

"As bad as that?"

"Something came up. Are you going to have a beer or not?"

"Not."

"Please yourself," he grunted.

"I will."

He took a sip of beer, looking at her over the brim of the glass. It was obvious he didn't much care for what he saw.

"Seeing we have to share this farm, we could

make a better job of sharing the work. Liked your morning out in the sun, did you?"

"It made a change from the office," she agreed.

"Perhaps you should try it more often. Your social life wouldn't suffer as mine has ever since you got here. After all, you're equally at home hobnobbing with the Maasai as you are with the Allans, isn't that so?"

"I suppose so," she murmured amicably. She didn't want to quarrel with him right now. It was enough for her that he hadn't enjoyed his morning with Felice nearly as much as he'd thought he would.

"I thought you might plead that dipping cattle isn't suitable work for a woman?"

"Is that what Felice told you?"

"You can leave her out of this!"

There was no doubt about it—he was in a thoroughly bad temper. Bar repressed a giggle.

"If you want me to see to the dipping, you have only to ask me nicely," she told him, pleased with herself and life in general. "With our own workers and the Maasai to help me, I'll manage very well."

He took another sip of beer. "It's only right you should pull your weight while you're here," he muttered.

Bar shot him a quick look. "Haven't I so far?"

"There's more to farming than filling in a few forms!"

"I see," Bar observed dryly. She could almost hear Felice speaking in his words. "Would you rather have the government on your back for not filling them in?"

"We managed before you came."

"I'm glad you think so!"

"Felice would have done them while she's here."

"Of course!" Bar exclaimed. "I'd forgotten Felice! She would have known exactly how to put the office in order. Her French and Italian would have been just the thing for the task. I wonder what 'tsetse fly' is in French?"

Jonathan frowned at her. "Why don't you like Felice? I believe you're jealous of her."

"You've got to be joking!"

His jaw clenched in anger. "She hasn't had your advantages of an English education, is that it? All the more credit to her for always looking as smart as paint!"

Bar felt her good humour slipping away from her. "When's the wedding to be?" she asked.

He stared at her for a long moment. "Is it her failed marriage that makes you feel so superior?"

"I don't feel superior!" Bar denied.

"It doesn't stop you from minding everyone else's business however you feel. Your father being my partner doesn't give you the right to interfere in my social life!"

"Nor you in mine!"

"You can invite your Maasai friends any time, they don't bother me! But you've hardly gone out of your way to make *my* guests welcome!"

She tilted her chin, her eyes hardening. "I don't much enjoy being made to feel unwelcome in my own house!"

"I keep telling you, it's not your house!"

"It was my father's, wasn't it?"

"He built it," Jonathan acknowledged. "It was always considered part of the farm before you came!"

"Well, it isn't working out now!" Bar retorted, now as angry as he. "One of us is going to have to move out, because I'll tell you here and now, I won't share it with Felice."

"How generous of you! You're as spoilt as your mother was before you. If you think I'm going to move out for your sake, you've got another think coming, Miss High-and-Mighty. If anyone builds, it's going to be you! You can have your pick of sites, just as long as it's well out of sight of *my* windows. Then, when you throw in the sponge and take yourself back to civilisation, I won't have to witness your retreat!"

Bar flung herself down into a chair, glowering at him and managing to look surprisingly like her father at the same time. Jonathan had never noticed much resemblance between father and daughter before. Now the similarity between Bob Nelson and his daughter was a speaking likeness. One could be every bit as stubborn as the other.

"I'll see you in court first!" she flung at him.

"We may come to that yet."

"We'll certainly come to that if you expect me to share this house with another woman!"

"Another woman, or Felice?"

"Felice is the only other woman around."

Jonathan finished his beer in a single gulp. "You'll want to get married yourself sooner or later. Shouldn't you give some thought to your reputation? Or are Englishmen prepared to share their women with their other lovers?"

"At the moment I don't have a lover at all," Bar said with dignity.

"Try telling that to anyone round here!" he dared her.

So that was what was eating him, Bar surmised. Felice didn't like him sharing a house with some other female.

"Have you tried?" she asked him innocently.

"Alice warned you how it would be if you didn't take her up on her offer to have you over there. It's natural for everyone to think you're sharing my bed as well as my house."

"You mean Felice thinks so?"

He shrugged his shoulders. "Your reputation will suffer more than mine! People out here don't admire promiscuity in a woman."

Bar laughed out loud. "Look who's talking. At least I don't get myself engaged to one man while I'm still married to another."

"I've told you before, we're not engaged!"

"What are you waiting for?"

He looked at his empty glass in a moody silence. "Don't you care what people think of you?" he asked at last.

"Not a whit!"

"Felice is hardly likely to keep quiet about it when she gets back to Nairobi," he warned her.

"Are you worried about me or about yourself?"

"You," he said abruptly. "Your father would have hated there to be any more talk about the Nelson women. It wasn't much fun for him when your mother left him."

"It wasn't a bundle of laughs for me either," Bar remembered.

His look was one of open contempt. "Don't you ever think of anyone but yourself? You could step back into your old life any time you chose, but his whole existence came crashing about his ears."

Bar flexed her fingers thoughtfully. "Okay, so what do you want me to do about it now? I don't think Felice is the sort of person who'd believe me if I told her I wasn't sharing your bed, do you? Most people judge other people by themselves."

He leaned towards her, holding his empty glass so tightly she expected it to disintegrate under the pressure. "What d'you mean by that?" he demanded.

"What should I mean except that I'm choosey as to who shares my bed?"

He snapped his fingers under her nose. "If I wanted to, what makes you think you could keep me out?"

"Because I wouldn't want you! I don't even like you."

His eyes met hers and the message she read there shattered what was left of her composure. Did he know the effect he had on her? She tore her gaze away, the effort of it making her breathless. How dare he challenge her in that way when he was more than half-engaged to another woman?

"I could make you want me," he said slowly.

Bar jumped to her feet and started across the verandah towards the french windows. "You flatter yourself!" she threw at him over her shoulder. "I think I'll have a cold drink after all."

Chapter Seven

"*Hodi!* Is anyone in?"

"Michael!" Bar's surprise showed in her voice as she darted out of the office to meet the son of the Allan household. "Michael, I thought you were in England!"

"I'm here for a couple of weeks. It breaks up the winter and I like to see the parents once every year at least."

"I'm glad to see you whatever the reason," Bar said warmly. I can't tell you how nice it is to see a friendly face!"

"Aren't the natives friendly?"

"Don't be silly, of course they are. It's my father's partner."

"You can win him over if you try!"

"I'm not trying," Bar denied. "I'm standing on my

rights. I'm my father's daughter and he left his share of the farm to me, and here I mean to stay."

"So your mother said," Michael Allan said slowly. "Not biting off more than you can chew, are you?"

Bar raised her chin. "Why should he have it all?"

"It's his livelihood."

"It's mine too!"

"It isn't the same for a girl. You'll marry and go and live with your husband. What else has this poor guy got?"

Bar forced a smile. "A near-fiancée. Hasn't your mother told you about her?"

Michael whistled softly. "Not Felice?"

Bar nodded. "Have you met her?"

"Last time I was here. A dishy bit of goods, but I thought she had a husband in the offing."

"Not for much longer." Bar sighed, unaware that she had done so. "Let's go inside, it's hot out here. What will you have? Tea? Something stronger? You'll stay and dine with us, won't you?"

Michael was disapproving. "Us?"

"We're both living here at the moment."

"Just as well your mother doesn't know that! Heavens above, Bar, my parents would put you up any time you asked, you know that. You can't stay on here with only a spare man to keep you company."

"As we're partners, I don't have much choice," Bar said dryly.

"Of course you have a choice! Shall I have a word with him?"

"He'll take advantage—"

"He's far more likely to take advantage of your being here alone with him," Michael protested.

Bar chuckled. "Don't judge others by yourself!" She couldn't count the number of times Michael had teased her by offering to take her away from all her troubles when she had lived with her mother. He never meant a word of it, of course, but once or twice, when he kissed her, she wondered if, one day, she might not come to care for him. At least he could talk to her about Kenya and the things they had shared and done in their childhood.

She led the way into her father's sitting room. It was a large, untidy room, the walls of undressed stone and the floors littered with the skins of animals, a relic from the times when it was considered quite respectable to shoot wild animals with guns rather than cameras. On her father's desk, still cluttered with his private papers, stood a folder with two photographs: Bar at twelve on one side, and her mother's laughing face on the other. Michael picked it up and looked at it.

"Funny, I don't remember your mother ever laughing when she lived out here," he remarked.

"Nor do I," Bar agreed. "She really hated it here."

"She rather hopes you will too, now you're grown up and have seen a bit of life in other places."

"This is the only place I've ever felt at home."

Michael laughed shortly. "I never feel at home here. Don't you ever long for a good museum?"

"There's one in Nairobi."

"It's hardly the Victoria and Albert, or the British Museum."

"No, but they'll still be there whenever I visit London. I can visit there just as often as you come here."

"I suppose so." Michael seated himself on the sofa beside her. "Your mother sent her love by the way."

"Did you go and see her specially?" Bar asked him. Michael and her mother got along very well indeed.

"As a matter of fact, I did. I wanted to assure her I'd look out for your interests while I was here. It sounds as though you need looking after too! Whatever made you agree to live under the same roof as Jonathan Grant?"

"I didn't think I had the right to throw him out, though it might come to that. This was my father's house and now it's mine, and that's all there is to it."

"He hasn't tried anything yet, then?"

"Tried what?"

Michael stirred uneasily. "Bar, you're not *fond* of him, are you?"

"Not particularly."

"Well, at least I can tell your mother that. She'd throw a fit if she knew how things really are. If you want to stay on here, though, you'll have to make some other arrangement. You'll soon find yourself recalled to England if you don't!"

Bar looked at Michael's nice, rather dull face and found herself comparing it in her mind's eye with a quite different one, one with a broken nose and a scar on his brow. She had no difficulty deciding which one she preferred and wondered how she could be so perverse when Michael was obviously the better man.

"That won't happen," she said cheerfully. "Clive wants my mother to himself. Besides, I'm a grown-up lady in case you hadn't noticed and nobody can recall me anywhere. I have a right to live where I want to."

"You're as stubborn as your father!"

"I'm his daughter."

"It's nothing to be proud of," he rebuked her. "If you ask me, this farm has a jinx on it. It broke up your parents' marriage, and it'll ruin your life too, if you let it. There isn't a patch of land in the world that's worth it."

"It is, if you love the land, if it's a part of you."

Michael gave her an angry look. "You're kidding yourself! You don't need a farm, you need a romance."

"Is that why you're here?"

"One of the reasons. I promised your mother—"

Bar shook her head at him. "That was where you made your mistake. I make my own decisions these days."

"You're too independent by half!"

"Too bad," said Bar, "because that's the way I like it." She smiled suddenly. "Now that we've got that over, d'you think we could talk about something else?"

Michael went on sitting there, considering what to say next: "You know I've always been fond of you," he went on at last. "We go well together. I can't think why you won't see reason and come back to England with me. You'll get lonely out here by yourself. Every woman needs some man to see she's all right in the end. There's no one for you out here, love."

Bar ground her teeth angrily. "Isn't there just!"

She saw the dawning light of understanding in his eyes and wished the words unsaid. How could she be so stupid as to give him a handle like that to beat her with? The news would be with her mother the very next time Michael saw her, and her mother would never let the matter rest. Why, she might even take the very next plane out from England to see what was going on! She wouldn't easily see her cherished plans for her daughter go down the drain.

"What about Felice?" Michael accused her doggedly.

"What about her?"

"I thought you said she was about to be engaged to Grant?"

Bar nodded. "That's right."

Michael turned this over in his mind. He had never been a quick thinker but, it seemed to Bar, he was being slower than ever today.

"Then you must be hanging on here, hoping he'll change his mind?"

Was that what she was doing? Bar certainly hoped not. "My dear Michael, you *have* been talking to my mother! Not content with getting herself married, nothing will do as far as she's concerned but to see me settled also. I'm too busy to think about such things just now. Jonathan might be willing to have me as a sleeping partner, but I mean to run this farm myself! I've been trained to do just that after all!"

Michael merely looked shocked. "Are you sleeping with him?" he demanded.

"Of course not!"

"There's no 'of course' about it! Mother says he can take his pick of any girl in Kenya, and you must be very vulnerable, living in his house."

"*My* house!"

He regarded her stubbornly set jaw and tried a

new tack. "He can't be such a good farmer himself,"
he remarked.

Bar's eyes flew to his face. "Why not?"

"Tikipit came to see me as soon as he heard I was
here. He tells me they're all going in fear of their
children's lives because of a half-tame lioness. He
wants me to shoot it for them. If they liked and
trusted Grant, wouldn't they have asked him to get
rid of the beast for them?"

Bar's spirits sank into her boots. "Maybe."

Michael pressed home his advantage. "It'd be
easier for him to get a licence—the Maasai must
know that."

Bar's lips quivered. "Do you think it's Father's
lion?"

"The one that killed him?"

She nodded, her eyes bright with unshed tears.

"Could be. He was a fool not to return her to the
wild, or else train her properly. Your father was
always eccentric, but he wasn't stupid. Perhaps he
had more of a death wish than any of us realised."

Bar stood up, averting her face from him. "What
are you going to do?"

Michael grunted. "I'm not going to Nairobi to
pick up a licence! The Maasai are more than capable
of getting rid of her by themselves if she's turned
into a maneater. More likely, she's just hungry and
unsure how to hunt for herself. She may learn if
she's left alone."

Bar wondered if Michael was a good enough judge
to tell, but she said nothing more on the subject.
Instead, she suggested a beer and went into the
kitchen to open a chilled can for him. She would try
to forget all about the lioness, she told herself, but

she knew she wouldn't be able to. She felt responsible for her father's actions because she was his daughter. She couldn't expect to inherit only the assets he had left behind him, and if something had to be done about his lioness it was up to her to see that it was done.

Did that mean telling Jonathan about it? The ring on the beer can slipped between her fingers. Why hadn't the Maasai told him of their fears? Did they consider him as much an outsider as she did? Had they decided that Michael was the one to tell because, although he didn't live there any longer, he had been born and brought up amongst them, as she had herself? Jonathan was the outsider, the odd man out. Jonathan was the one who'd be a stranger to them until he died!

The can opened with a rush, spilling some of the beer on the floor. Bar poured what was left into a glass and searched under the sink for a cloth to clear up the mess. She didn't hear Jonathan come in and the first she knew of his presence was when she came face to face with his polished boots a few inches away from her nose.

"Is that beer for me?" he enquired.

"It's for Michael!"

"It didn't take him long to get over here," Jonathan commented in even tones. "Are you the reason he's paying his parents one of his rare visits?"

Bar sat back on her heels. "He comes every year."

"Some years."

"Fat lot you know about it!" Bar said rudely. "I've known Michael all my life and he's not the sort of person who'd neglect his parents. I can't say the same for you, of course."

"My parents are dead. If they were running a farm far too big for them to manage as they got older, I wouldn't be here having to suffer you as a constant thorn in my side! Are you having a beer too?"

"No."

Jonathan kicked the floorcloth out of her reach. "Don't let me stop you taking your boyfriend his. I'm sure he can't wait for you to get back to him!"

Bar cast him a look of pure hatred. "Michael's not my boyfriend!"

"He'd like to be, is that it?"

"I've known him all my life. He's a friend, that's all." She picked up the beer and stormed out of the kitchen without a backward look. "Not that it's any business of yours," she added under her breath.

Jonathan's hand came down on her shoulder. For a big man, he could move more quickly than anyone else she knew.

"While you're here, Barbara Nelson, it's very much my business. *Everything* you do is my business! Everything!" he said again with a grim humour she preferred to ignore.

"How d'you work that out?"

"It's my business to keep this farm together."

"You take too much on yourself!"

"I don't think so."

"You wouldn't!"

She would have argued the point further with him, but he picked up the two glasses of beer and walked out, leaving her to finish clearing up the kitchen floor.

By the time she joined the two men in the sitting room they were deep in conversation. Jonathan made a better host than she had supposed, she noticed sourly. He went out of his way to make himself agreeable to Michael, turning the conversation into channels which he knew would interest him and listening to Michael's long, rather pompous pronouncements on world affairs, as though agreeing with him right down the line.

Bar threw in the occasional remark of her own, but she had heard Michael on his favourite topic of conversation more than once before and she was hard put to it to pretend an interest she was far from feeling.

"Are you going into politics, Michael?" she asked at last.

"I may." He hesitated. "Your mother thinks I ought to get married first. A suitable wife would be a great help to me." A gleam entered his eyes. "Interested?"

"Not in politics," she answered him.

"Your mother is."

"I'm not my mother."

"You must have inherited something from her," he protested.

"I did. I look like her."

"In a way," Michael agreed. "Though you don't look much like her dressed like that! She's always perfectly turned out."

"It means a lot to her," Bar said on a laugh. "You know it means nothing at all to me."

Michael smiled teasingly at her. "You forget how long I've know you, Bar dear. You'll grow more and more like your mother as you get older. Life out here won't satisfy you for ever. You'll be yearning to do something else before long. Your father's way of life was all right when you were twelve, but you'll soon need more than a few wild animals to keep you company."

"She has the Maasai," Jonathan put in.

Michael repressed a shudder. "They taught her Maa when she was a child. The rest of us found it too difficult, but not Bar! Her nurse was a Maasai woman."

"She still speaks Maa," Jonathan confirmed.

Michael looked disgruntled. "Still? Who to?"

"Gazelles amongst other things," Jonathan told him laughing.

"It's more useful out here than in England," Bar said dryly. "Most of my talents are."

Michael finished his beer. "You'll never convince me of that, sweetheart. Or your mother either." He put his empty glass down on the table by her side. "Coming to see me off?"

She rose reluctantly, very much aware of Jonathan watching her every movement. Even with Michael there, Michael whom she had known all her life, it was Jonathan of whom she was conscious. She didn't have to look at him to see his hard, tanned body, and every time she moved she was remembering how it felt to be held close against him and to be kissed by him. It brought a heat to her body such as Michael had never been able to inspire.

She went with him out onto the verandah, a smile pinned to her lips, though she didn't feel like smiling at all. She couldn't understand herself at all. Why couldn't it be Michael who made her feel like a woman and not Jonathan?

"I'm glad you're here, Michael," she said aloud, trying to make herself believe it was true.

"Are you? You didn't seem to be much interested in all my news."

She wrinkled up her nose. "I can't help not being interested in politics, can I?"

"You haven't tried!"

She shrugged her shoulders. "They seem so far away. I'm sorry, Michael."

He put a friendly arm about her shoulders. "You'll change your mind before very long. I'm relying on it. I promised your mother—"

"She should have known better than to ask you," Bar said with disapproval.

"She only wants you to be happy. That's all we both want for you!"

"I'm happy here," she said abruptly.

Michael pulled her close against him. "You may think you are, Bar, but that's only because you're such an innocent. What will you do when Jonathan marries and you have to clear out? You'd do much better coming home with me now."

Bar sighed. How often did she have to say it? "I am at home! Home has always been here for me!"

"With Jonathan and wife?" he asked.

She bit her lip, knowing she had to convince herself of the answer to that question as much as she had to convince him.

"It's my house and my farm," she said.

It was a gentle kiss Michael gave her before he ran down the steps of the verandah to his parents' car. Bar pressed her lips together and waved her hand to him. The kiss had meant nothing, she knew that, but she could almost wish it had been something more than a casual salute between two old friends. Why couldn't Michael make her heart knock against her ribs and her spine tingle with that forbidden excitement that a single glance from Jonathan could inspire in her?

She turned back and went inside, considering the problem. Jonathan had opened himself another can of beer and was sitting spread-eagled on his chosen chair. The sight of him made her avert her eyes and brought the colour dancing to her cheeks. She wanted to touch him, to run a finger along the scar on his brow. She wanted him to kiss her, as Michael had kissed her, because he was fond of her and wanted to give her pleasure.

"I thought you might go with him?" Jonathan drawled from his chair.

"I have things to do here."

"What things?"

"Little things," she said lightly, "like dipping the cattle."

"Ah yes, I've been thinking about that. I don't think your boyfriend would think it a proper job for you, do you?"

"Michael has nothing to do with it!" she exclaimed.

Jonathan sat up straight. "Are you sure?"

"Look, how many times do I have to tell you? Michael is a friend, nothing more."

"But he'd like to be?"

Bar glared at the seated man. She wanted to dislike him, she thought in despair, and all she could think of was how it would feel to run her fingers through his hair. She must be going mad!

"So?" she demanded.

He stood up, looking down his nose at her. The fact that his nose wasn't as straight as it once had been only added to the attraction his face had for her. She wrenched her eyes away from his, hoping he wouldn't notice that her breathing was agitated, and that she couldn't find anything satisfactory to do with her hands. It was a forlorn hope at best, for she knew him to be an observant man.

"Your mother may be a better ally to your heart than you gave me to understand. If we're to be partners, I want to know where I stand."

"Exactly where you've always stood! It's none of your business what I do. You wouldn't be asking me all these questions if I were a man, would you?"

His mouth quirked into a smile. "You're not a man," he pointed out.

"I know that!" she snorted.

"I imagine you might. Allan would hardly kiss you like that if you were."

"You've kissed me too!"

"Right, I have. So we're agreed you're not a man and that neither of us is likely to treat you like one. Where does that get us?"

"Back where we started, with me dipping the cattle and you minding your own business."

Jonathan's eyes narrowed dangerously. "Not quite, Miss Barbara Nelson. Michael Allan has no place on any farm of mine, whatever he means to you. He may be a whiz at his own profession, but as a farmer he's a nonstarter."

Bar had long ago come to the same conclusion, but she saw no reason to admit it to the arrogant, unpleasant man before her.

"Are you planning to choose my friends for me as well as ordering me about all the time?" she asked, drawing herself up to her full height.

"When it comes to anything to do with the farm, what I say goes," he retorted.

"We'll see about that!"

She turned on her heel and marched out to the office, which, more even than her bedroom, had become her place of refuge from the man she kept telling herself she hated and despised. Once there, she sat down with her head in her hands. What a silly quarrel it was! As if she would allow Michael anywhere near the farm. She knew what he was like, what he had always been like in all the years she had known him. He rode badly, he was frightened of any animal on four feet, including her mother's pet dogs, and he had no feeling for the land whatsoever. No, what nagged at her was that Jonathan should trust her judgement so little as to think she might discuss the farm with Michael. She might with his parents, but they were experienced farmers and loved the land as she did.

The door of the office banged open and Jonathan's large frame stood in the doorway.

"Did you understand what I said? I'll see to the dipping of the cattle. You can see to the house and the office."

"And miss all the fun?"

"If you like."

She jerked back in her chair. "But why?"

"Because I won't have your 'friend' anywhere near my cattle at such a time. He'd be sure to stampede the lot, or worse, and his mother and father are friends of mine."

"What makes you think Michael would want to spend a hot, dusty day dipping your cattle? Not even for my sake—"

"You underrate yourself!"

She tried staring him out of countenance. Of a sunny disposition, she couldn't remember having lost her temper so completely and so often with anyone else as she had with Jonathan.

"I don't want Michael going back to my mother with any tales about us," she explained with a sort of numb desperation. "The only way to convince him that nothing's going on between us is to let him come and go as he likes. I'll see that he doesn't get in the way. You don't have to worry."

Jonathan laid his hands down flat on the desk in front of her. "It's important that we get the Maasai cattle through the dip this year. Michael Allan unsettles them." He took a deep breath. "You can have your fun some other time."

Bar didn't believe a word of it. If Michael upset them, they wouldn't have told him about the man-eating lioness, they would have told Jonathan.

"Michael was brought up amongst the Maasai, which is more than you were!" she shot back at him. "They've always liked and trusted him!"

"Have they?"

Bar's temper, always uncertain where this man was concerned, flared and caught fire. She lifted a hand, intending to strike the complacent face that was far too close to her own, but he moved swiftly, catching her wrist and forcing her arm behind her back.

"You won't miss his kisses as much as you think." His words struck her ears like pebbles against a pane of glass. "Any man will do for that, Barbara Nelson!"

She felt herself lifted out of her chair and hard up against the edge of the desk and his shoulders.

"Go away!" she screamed at him.

But his mouth came down on hers just the same and she couldn't hide from herself any longer that it wasn't anger with him she felt, it was something quite different, and it was this something that gave him the last word, leaving her weak and breathless under the onslaught of his kiss.

"You won't miss him at all!" he said as he pushed her back into her chair. She heard his laughter as he left the room.

Chapter Eight

It took Bar some time to get the hang of the radio-telephone that linked neighbour to distant neighbour in the vast countryside. She supposed it had always been there, lurking in a recess in the office, but she had never been called upon to use it in her childhood and she was too proud to ask Jonathan for instructions on how to work it now. It had a way of crackling and allowing the voice of the person on the other end to disappear altogether at intervals, and she didn't know if she should retune the set or what.

It was an easy way of talking to Michael without Jonathan's knowledge, however. Bar didn't want her father's partner to know how often Michael got in touch with her, often getting through only to say good morning or good night. She was all the more annoyed therefore, while she was struggling to get some sense out of the instrument, when Jonathan came in and took it out of her hands.

"Trying to get hold of Nairobi?" he asked her.

Such an idea had never occurred to her. Had he been in touch with his solicitor? Should she have been in touch with her father's, just in case he was still working on some way of getting rid of her?

"The Allans."

"Ah!"

Bar had simply wanted to complain of being left behind once again. She had always enjoyed the excitement of a cattle dip and she resented her exclusion from the first one to be held on her own land. She didn't know why she didn't just saddle a horse and ride out, no matter what Jonathan had said to her, but she knew she didn't dare without encouragement from someone. Michael, she thought, would be the person to supply her with ammunition to take on Jonathan when she finally got her own way.

"I thought I'd ask them to dinner," she explained off the top of her head.

"Did you now?"

His disbelief nettled her. "Just because we're not getting on at the moment is no excuse for being thoroughly unsociable to everyone else as well," she murmured primly.

"I thought we were getting on pretty well," Jonathan remarked smugly, switching on the radio-telephone with all of his usual calm competence.

Bar looked at him with mounting resentment. "How did you come to that conclusion?"

"The farm's working smoothly, we haven't openly quarrelled recently, and you've shown sufficient sense to keep away from the cattle dip when I told you to."

"It had nothing to do with you!" Bar retorted.

His eyebrows shot up. "No?"

"If I'd made up my mind to go, I'd have gone, whatever you said about it!"

He grinned at her, and she wondered how he managed to look so completely at home half-sitting on her desk. He looked as if he belonged there and she was annoyed because she welcomed his presence in spite of herself. It was unreasonable that she should get so much pleasure from looking at someone she thoroughly disliked, or would dislike if she had better control over the excessive excitement of her flesh whenever it came into contact with him.

"I almost wish you had! I enjoy doing battle with you every now and then."

There was no dignified answer she could make to that. She glowered at him with disapproval, trying not to imagine what he would have done if she had ridden out to watch the cattle being dipped.

She looked down her nose. "Are you going to do battle over my dinner party?"

"No." He stood up. "Ask whom you like."

She sighed when he had gone. If he didn't want her to give a dinner party, why didn't he say so? She thought he liked the Allans, who weren't at all the kind of people to jump to conclusions because Bar insisted on staying in her father's house. She had explained her reasons to them, and while she knew that Michael didn't approve, his parents had been remarkably understanding.

She read the instructions for the radio-telephone once again, making it the third time, and realised her thoughts strayed far from the pages before her. She was remembering every detail of Jonathan's appearance, the way his hair grew out of his scalp and the hardness of his muscles, anything and everything that made him different from any other man she had ever known—especially Michael.

The thought brought a smile to her lips. Poor Michael! Even in a dinner jacket, something he wore as often as Jonathan wore his riding boots, he would look a pale shadow of a man beside his reluctant host. Jonathan's masculinity was something no female could ignore, but Michael had never been more than a friend to her anyway and never would be.

To her surprise she managed to get through to the Allans quite easily. She must have taken in more of the instructions than she had supposed. She rather hoped it would not be Michael who answered, and in that she was lucky for it was Mrs. Allan's voice that came weakly over the wire.

"Alice Allan speaking. Over."

"It's me, Bar."

Mrs. Allan sounded amused. "At a guess I'd say you're not used to using this contraption. If you don't say 'over,' I don't know when to switch my lever over so that I can say something."

Bar flicked her own lever, glad to learn at last what that cliché meant.

"I wanted to ask you all over to dinner tomorrow. Over," she announced.

"All of us? Over."

"Please. Over."

"Not just Michael? Over."

Had Alice noticed how often her son had got through to Bar in the last few days? She hoped not.

Because he had dropped by whenever he wanted to while she was living with her mother, Michael seemed to think that he was in some way special to her. The time was coming when she would have to tell him that there could never be anything warmer than friendship between them. He thought of her as her mother's daughter, who would shortly come to her senses and return to the kind of life her mother lived, but in that he was doomed to disappointment. Politics and cocktail parties bored her rigid. In fact Michael bored her too.

"Certainly not just Michael!" she exclaimed.

There was a pause and then Alice Allan said, "Poor Michael. Okay, dear, we'll all come. Shall we dress? Over."

"Do you usually? Over." At least she had remembered the "over" this time.

"Yes. We don't have many opportunities to get all dolled up," Mrs. Allan confirmed. "We'll be along at about half past six. Will Jonathan be there? Over."

"Of course," said Bar. She didn't want to say anything more about Jonathan, not then. "Over and out," she added triumphantly and cut off the power. She hadn't needed Jonathan after all to show her how to use the radio-telephone! She didn't need him for anything!

But she did need Solomon to help her cook the dinner. She could manage the charcoal fire well enough, but it was hard to be cook and hostess as well, so Solomon must put the last-minute touches to the food and carry it into the dining room. She could remember, when she was a child, Solomon dressing himself up in black trousers and an embroidered scarlet waistcoat, together with a Muslim cap for his head, and serving at table whenever her parents gave a party. He always enjoyed such occasions, as she did, for her mother gave the best parties of anyone she knew.

In those days there was no deep-freeze. Now, when Solomon opened it up for her inspection, Bar was amazed at the various cuts of meat that were stored away, together with vegetables and fruits, some from as far away as England.

"Don't we grow vegetables anymore?" Bar asked Solomon.

"Bwana Nelson said it was too much trouble."

"Trouble? In land you only have to dip your fingernails into to have them grow?"

Solomon looked suitably chastened. "My wife keeps a garden going for us. If you want fresh vegetables tomorrow—"

Bar refused his kind offer, for there was so much in stock, ready for her use. That was another job about to come under her sphere of influence, she decided. She would have a vegetable garden marked out for her in the morning and would plant it before Jonathan heard of it.

Perhaps it was the digging that left her feeling tired and listless the following evening. She showered, washed her hair, and changed into a cotton caftan of a vivid royal blue she knew she looked well in, and then went to check on the drinks she had asked Solomon to set out on the verandah. Jonathan was there before her. His dinner jacket was of cream linen over extremely well-fitting black trousers. He looked magnificent and, worse still, completely at home in formal dress. It was only then that she realised she had been hoping he would look as out of place as Michael did on the back of a horse.

"Very nice!" he complimented her.

She was tempted to return the compliment. Indeed, she opened her mouth to do so before she changed her mind, looking down at her bare toes in evening sandals instead.

"If you didn't look so solemn, we'd look like an old married couple," he teased her. "Will you have a drink while we're waiting?"

She shook her head, muttering about having to see how the meal was getting on in the kitchen. Her heart was pounding as she gained the corridor, and she leaned against the wall for a minute to catch her breath. The weariness that had afflicted her earlier was gone, but she was convinced she was sickening for something all the same. She was hot and cold by turns and—and she wanted Jonathan! She wanted to run into his arms and feel the hardness of his embrace and the strength of his kiss! She had to be going mad!

"Feeling better?" he asked her as she retraced her steps slowly out onto the verandah.

"I feel fine, thank you," she answered, her head high.

A smile touched the corners of his mouth. "Are you sure you didn't spend too long in the sun?"

She frowned at him. "I'm as tough as old boots!" she assured him. "I may come out with you tomorrow." Her eyes didn't quite meet his and she had no warning when his hand came up to grasp her arm. "Let go of me!" she said sharply.

"Why don't you let your hair hang free?" he asked her.

She slanted a look at him, unsure of herself and him. "I prefer it out of my way."

"Because it makes you look older and more sophisticated?"

"That too," she admitted.

"I prefer you young and vulnerable."

He smiled down at her, closer than she had realised. "Do you mind?" he said, and he took the pins from her hair, collecting them carefully together and putting them away in his pocket. Her hair fell in a haphazard curtain about her face and she brushed it angrily away, pushing it back behind her shoulders.

"Yes, I do mind!"

He bent his head and kissed the tip of her nose. "No, you don't," he said against her ear. "You want to look beautiful for me."

"For you or Michael?"

He released her with a suddenness that made her stumble. "Have it your own way," he said and went out onto the drive to greet their guests.

Feeling unaccountably depressed, Bar surveyed her dinner guests and wondered why she should have gone to all the trouble of asking them. Take Michael, for one, who had proved as unsatisfactory a foil to Jonathan as she had thought he would be, which increased her displeasure with the man who sat at the head of the table, looking more like the perfect host of her imagination every minute.

"What have you been doing with yourself, my dear?" Alice Allan asked her. "We expected you over more often, especially with Michael at home."

Bar raised a smile. "I've been working for my living. First the office, and now I'm trying to do something about a vegetable garden. Would you believe we only have frozen vegetables on the table tonight?"

"So that's what all the digging was about," Jonathan said. "No wonder you look tired. This dinner party is more your scene than digging up the African dust! Isn't this what you've been missing ever since you left England?"

"If you want to think so." Bar clamped her mouth shut, regarding the food on her plate with disfavour. Whatever she did was wrong as far as Jonathan was concerned. There was no way she was ever going to persuade him that she was where she wanted to be, so she might just as well please herself! "If I'm tired it's because I've been stuck here in the house these last few days. I don't care what you say, I'm riding out to the cattle dip tomorrow. Why don't you join us, Michael?"

If Michael recognised the urgency in her voice, he gave no sign of it.

"Don't be daft, love. I'm here on holiday, remember?"

"But, Michael—"

He shook his head. "You ought to know by this time that I haven't the stomach for such occupations. The most I'll do is fly out in the light aeroplane, bringing a picnic with me. I guarantee I'll keep you well fed and entertained all afternoon! How's that?"

Bar didn't have to look at Jonathan to know what he would be thinking of that offer. "Anyone who comes will have to do his share of the work," she muttered. "Except Jonathan. He's already done his share, rounding up the cattle with the Maasai. He can stay at home if he likes."

She eyed him through her lashes, waiting for him to lose his temper, but he always had himself very well under control. Far from showing any anger, he was actually smiling.

"What makes you think you can manage without me?" he asked languidly.

"I'll have Michael—" She broke off, horribly aware of the colour mounting in her cheeks. What good would Michael be to her? Besides, he wasn't the one she wanted. *She wanted Jonathan!* She pushed her hair back from her face, playing with it between her fingers. "It won't hurt to have a picnic, will it?"

Alice Allan looked from one to the other of them. "Why not?" she chimed in. "I'll get some food together and send it with Michael. He can take the plane, can't he, Peter?"

Mr. Allan nodded. "No good expecting Michael to do any real farming though," he added. "Michael's like your mother, my dear, only happy when he's with a lot of people all gabbling about nothing!"

His wife put a restraining hand on his arm. "Michael's very good at theory," she said gently.

Peter Allan repeated the word explosively. "He tells a lot of other people who don't know a thing about it what they expect to hear. Last time I was in England I heard one of his lectures. Meant to be about African politics, wasn't it, lad? Nonsense, the whole lot of it!"

"That's because you don't move with the times,"

his son told him shortly. "You're too close to things in Africa to see them as they really are."

Peter Allan exchanged glances with Jonathan, the sympathy between them totally lacking between father and son.

"You've never understood what Africa is about," the father said wearily. "Giving everything a label that means something to Europeans, doesn't mean it has any relevance out here. That's the mistake we've always made. Capital versus labour means something in Europe, it's land which matters out here. You talk as if everywhere south of the Equator was suffering from the same problems and trot out the solutions regardless of what's actually happening on the ground. You should make a very good politician!"

Michael ground his teeth. "I didn't get my degree for nothing!"

"You certainly didn't get it for what you know about farming the land either. I'd sooner leave my land to my workers than to you!"

Bar, thoroughly cross with both men, valiantly tried to turn the conversation into safer channels. "Why don't you all come out for the picnic tomorrow?" she asked them brightly.

It was Alice Allan who answered her. "No, my dear, that wouldn't be fair to Jonathan. He'll want to get the dip over as quickly as possible and we'd only be in the way."

Bar said nothing more. When they went into the sitting room, she served the coffee with her own hands, accepting Michael's compliment on her new hairstyle as if she hadn't heard him. She wished she hadn't asked him to go anywhere with her. If he did get in the way, Jonathan would be furious and he would be right. If she wanted to stay, the farm had to come before her social life, as it did, deep down, only she wanted to get a rise out of Jonathan, to show him that she might have to accept him as her partner, as he had been her father's, but she certainly wasn't going to accept him as boss. It was not a good start to have Michael flipping about in his father's light aeroplane and making a nuisance of himself. And he would, of course. She knew from experience how quickly Michael got bored with anything to do with the land and how he was bound to try some stunt like stampeding the cattle. When they had been children, only her mother would laugh when he disrupted the work of both farms, but she knew better than her mother that his tricks weren't funny but were sometimes dangerous. Only how was she to persuade Jonathan of that now?

"Why don't you come to us for a long visit until you've got everything sorted out?" Alice's voice broke into her unhappy thoughts.

"It's my place to be here," she said stubbornly.

"What does Jonathan think about that? He has all of the professional's contempt for the amateur, you know."

Bar, acknowledging the truth of that, asked, "Do you think Michael's an amateur?"

"As a farmer, my dear, I'd have thought it was obvious. He earns a very nice living from his university as an academic, though."

Bar would have preferred not to have the issue put so baldy. They weren't the only two men in the world! But even as she was telling herself so, she was already thinking, no, Jonathan is the only man in the world for me! But how could she be so craven as to submit to all his prejudices just because she was wildly attracted to him?

"I'd die if I had to go back to England, Alice. My mother blossomed, but I died a little each day away from my roots. It would be worse this time!"

"Because of Jonathan?"

But Bar wasn't prepared to admit anything of the kind, not even to this kindly woman whom she'd known all her life.

"Because this is my home," she said.

When the Allans had gone, Bar lingered on the verandah, trying to make up her mind to apologise to Jonathan for inviting Michael to join the cattle dip the next day.

"I'm sorry, Jonathan," she began uncomfortably.

"So you should be. Michael Allan has as little idea of how to live out here as your mother had!"

"You never knew my mother."

"I feel I'm getting to know her better every day," Jonathan assured her.

Bar moved closer to him, her head bent so that her hair effectively hid her face from him. "I'm not really like her, you know," she said.

"No?"

She shook her head. The unaccustomed bulk of her hair about her shoulders bothered her and she pushed it impatiently out of her way. It was important to her that she should convince him that she belonged exactly where she was and nowhere else.

"It's difficult to explain what I mean, but I can breathe out here. In England it's all very pretty, but there's always a small, rounded hill, or a house, or something in the way of the view. The scenery is all very tame and domesticated—no grandeur anywhere. I starved for a view across the plains and the sight of a distant rainstorm and the mountains."

She thought his expression softened, but she could have been mistaken.

"That may have mattered to you when you were a child, but there's very little social life out here to suit you. The gentlemen farmers have all sold out long ago."

"Why should that matter to me?"

The scar shone very white on his brow, and before she could stop herself she put up a hand and traced it with her forefinger as she had so often longed to do.

"There are no Michaels here to entertain you, Miss Nelson, and my ways would fall far short of your exacting standards. To live in a wild land might entertain you for a while, to live my kind of life day in day out wouldn't please you at all!"

Bar gave him look for look. "It will please Felice, I suppose?"

"She knows what to expect if she settles down here."

"And I don't?"

"Michael is only here for a fortnight in the year, if that."

Bar's lips trembled, though whether it was with laughter or tears it was hard to tell.

"I can live without Michael. He's just a friend."

Jonathan's hand whipped out, pinning her close up against him. "Does he know that? You're as heartless as your mother, Barbara Nelson! Encouraging a man with one breath, putting him down with the next. No girl of mine would ever get away with it!"

Bar's flesh tingled beneath his grasp. "Why do you despise Michael?" she asked. "And me?"

His hold tightened, bruising her arm. "I despise him because he follows you around like a pet dog, knowing you're going to throw him away in the end."

Bar gasped, the breath startled out of her. "And me?" she repeated.

"I don't think about you at all!"

She wrenched herself free, rubbing at her arm and wondering why it should matter to her what he thought.

"Michael is worth ten of you!" she declared at last. "At least he doesn't mind people knowing he has some emotions. You're nothing but a stuffed shirt!"

"Then you won't miss me when you're gone!"

"No. I won't." She tossed her head. "Michael knows more about what makes a woman tick than you ever will! I'd be a fool not to listen to anything he said. I'm very glad I asked him to come along tomorrow!"

Jonathan's grim expression frightened her. She edged her way round him, deciding suddenly to make for her bedroom and safety, but whichever way she tried to move she found his body blocking her way. She felt his hand in the small of her back, compelling her hard against him, hip to hip.

"So I don't understand women, don't I?" he breathed against her mouth. "I understand this game you're playing better than you do. Put Michael through any hoops you choose, but I only jump when I want to jump and not at any bidding of yours."

"The same goes for me!" she said proudly.

"Does it? Oh, does it?" he mocked her.

She raised her chin a fraction of an inch and his lips met hers, knocking the breath out of her body. A wave of pleasant anticipation rolled over her, weakening her will power and turning her knees to jelly.

"If Michael could make you feel like that you wouldn't be here with me now," he growled, nipping the lobe of her ear between his teeth. "Go to bed, my dear, while I'm still prepared to let you go alone!"

She felt cold and shivered slightly as he pushed her away. "And what would Felice have to say to that?" she countered, retreating to a safe distance. But she thought she knew the answer all the time. Felice wouldn't need to say anything because Jonathan already belonged to her and they understood each other perfectly. She had nothing to fear from a fool like Bar Nelson. Jonathan would already have assured her of that.

Chapter Nine

Bar was a good rider, but Jonathan was better. He sat his horse as though he were a part of it, guiding it with an ease Bar could only envy. She was handicapped by her mount being too large for her, but he was a good, solid horse who could carry her safely all day without tiring. She had been half expecting an argument that morning, but Jonathan said nothing at all beyond ensuring that her girth was tight enough and that she really did know what she was doing on a horse.

She fell back a short way behind him, watching his easy motion just ahead of her. It was a moment for daydreaming and Bar made the most of it. It was easy enough to imagine herself in his arms, harder to imagine herself as the one woman in the world for him. She sighed involuntarily.

Jonathan turned his head, slowing his mount so that she could catch up.

"Is the pace too fast for you?"

She reached her hand up to confirm that the single fat plait she had made of her hair was still in place. Her hat lurched to a dangerous angle and she had to concentrate on rescuing it and putting it back on.

"I'm enjoying myself," she told him. "It's so long since I've done anything like this. The early mornings are the best time of all, don't you think?"

"We've still got a long way to go," he warned her.

She nodded happily. "I thought I heard a lion hunting a moment ago, but it's not very likely round here, is it?"

When Jonathan looked concerned, she knew he was thinking of her father's killer, as she was herself. If the escaped lioness were out hunting, they would have been better off in some kind of a vehicle than on horseback.

"The Maasai were out hunting her the other day," she told him reluctantly.

"I know."

"You mean you've known all the time? I thought they were keeping it a secret from you."

"Now why," he asked dryly, "should they do that?"

There was only one reason and she couldn't possibly explain it to him. She assumed the Maasai didn't trust him, but it was beginning to look as though she was wrong. But why, if they had already asked Jonathan, would they also ask Michael to shoot the lioness? Had Jonathan refused them?

"I thought—" she began, embarrassed.

"I don't speak Maa, but we manage to live alongside one another. Your father didn't speak Maa either."

Bar felt uncomfortable under his level gaze. "At one time a Maasai wasn't fully a man until he'd killed a lion single-handed," she said. "The *moran* who spoke to me about it was on his way to kill her. He said she was threatening the children."

Jonathan dropped back until their horses were side by side. "Why didn't you tell me about it?"

"I didn't want her killed," she confessed.

"Better her than another human being."

"I don't believe she'd kill again!" Bar exclaimed. "She probably didn't mean to kill my father. It was an accident. Everyone said so."

"A predictable accident," Jonathan insisted. "I warned him a dozen times that he ought to do something about her. It doesn't do to be sentimental about wild animals. He knew more about lions than I shall ever know, but in this case he was wrong. Lions were meant to behave like lions, not like people. Personally, I like them better that way."

Bar wiped her brow on the back of her hand. She wasn't enjoying this conversation. Her sympathies lay with her father, although she knew Jonathan was right. If it had been any other animal, she would have wanted it to have the freedom to be itself, but this lion had been her father's.

"It wouldn't have happened if he hadn't been lonely."

"Whose fault was that?"

The sweat trickled down her spine. "You think it was mine, don't you?" she accused him.

Jonathan shrugged. "He needed someone of his own."

"I was coming as fast as I could! He had you!"

"I didn't belong to him. Your father was a possessive man. When I first teamed up with him, he would like to have looked on me as a son, but I'd only just escaped my own father. I wasn't ready for another, not if there were any strings attached. I wanted to be my own man and live my own life, free from any emotional commitments. He couldn't understand that. Can you?"

"I don't know anything about your life before you came here." She wanted to, though. She was eager for every detail she could gather about him. She wouldn't really be content until she knew everything about his life as well as she knew her own. Did that make her a possessive kind of person too?

"My mother died when I was born. My father never married again. On the rare occasions he wanted someone other than myself with him, he'd visit Nairobi and try to drink himself to death."

"Did you go with him?"

"I lived up on the Northern Frontier. When I grew up, I wanted to leave, but my father wouldn't hear of it. He'd reared me single-handed and I owed him, he reckoned. There wasn't much affection between us."

"What happened to him?" Bar asked, shocked by the loneliness Jonathan must have suffered as a boy.

"He died of cancer. It was a slow, painful death, but nothing would induce him to go to a doctor."

"What happened to you?"

"I was with him until he died. It was only then I discovered he was one of the richest men in Kenya and there was absolutely no reason why we should have lived as we did, with only dust and desert for company. I'm only glad I escaped before this recent cycle of droughts. We both would have died if we'd still been there."

Bar was silent. No wonder Jonathan didn't show his feelings easily. Perhaps he didn't have it in him to love any woman as she wanted to be loved. Was that why he had chosen to marry Felice, beautiful Felice, who would never feel anything much for anyone but herself?

She didn't want to think of Felice getting close to him. It hurt, like a physical pain somewhere in her middle. She eyed his strong profile, remembering how his scar had felt beneath her fingers.

"I would have come earlier if I'd known," she said aloud. "I thought I'd be more use to my father when I'd qualified in farm management." She was silent for a moment, waiting for him to speak, but he said nothing at all. "How did you get that scar?"

He cast her an amused glance. "I'll tell you one of these days."

"Why not now?"

"It might give you ideas," he answered promptly.

The reins slackened in her hands. "What ideas?"

"You may speak Maa," he remarked, "but you know very little of the language of love."

She was willing to learn, but she could hardly tell him as much. Instead, she averted her eyes from the thin white line on his brow and dug in her heels to get ahead of him. She'd like to sympathise with him over his awful youth too, but he didn't want her sympathy. He probably didn't want anyone's sympathy, counting it a weakness.

"I'll teach you Maa, if you like," she called back over her shoulder.

"And give away your one advantage?"

"I thought you were my partner," she answered.

"Maybe. I'll let you know when I've made up my mind about that."

She flashed a smile, hoping she looked more confident than she felt. She wished she could dislike him, anything rather than have him inhabit her mind and heart to the exclusion of anyone and anything else.

Bar was glad to see the cattle and the assembled Maasai before them. She moved towards them at a canter, waving her hat in the air, and the men stood on one leg like dignified storks, the other leg tucked up against their thighs, and waved their spears in the air.

At the same moment, Michael's light aeroplane flew overhead, dipping dangerously low over the herd and the frightened horses, before rising again, turning and coming round again to land.

"Young fool!" Jonathan said through his teeth.

"Michael's always been like that," Bar told him. "He doesn't mean any harm."

"Spoilt rotten," Jonathan murmured, shafting a look at her. "He thinks you admire him for it. Do you?"

"I like him," Bar compromised.

Jonathan suddenly looked very large on his horse. "If you don't want him, cut the sentiment and tell him so. He's done enough damage to his father's farm without starting on mine."

"What damage?" Bar demanded.

Jonathan sat very still. "You really don't know, do

you? He's mortgaged the Allan's farm up to the hilt to buy himself a fancy car. Peter is little more than manager now on his own farm."

Bar swallowed, her eyes wide. "Michael wouldn't —he couldn't! It wasn't his to give or sell, not without his father's consent."

"It became his years ago to save death duties."

He rode away, taking up a strategic position in the dust in case the cattle, frightened by the noise of the aeroplane's engines, should start to bolt. Bar turned her horse's head in the opposite direction, cursing Michael's thoughtlessness. A spurt of dust came up and hit her full in the face. She wiped the worst of the red earth away with one hand, blinking painfully and getting ready to tell him what she thought of him as soon as she could see again.

But it wasn't Michael who first stepped out of the Cessna. Bar couldn't fail to recognise the bleached, fair hair of Felice Arghetti. Dressed in an improbable pink jumpsuit, she looked better prepared for a walk down Bond Street than across the plains of Africa. Her makeup was perfect, her shoes high-heeled and as pink as her suit. She looked about her, shading her eyes from the sun with one pearl-tipped hand. She spotted Bar and flapped the same hand weakly in her direction.

"My dear, whatever happened? You look simply *awful!*"

"Your landing kicked up quite a lot of dust," Bar answered dryly.

"Too bad you were in the way."

"We were afraid the herd would run."

Felice brushed off her immaculate jumpsuit, relishing the contrast between herself and the decidedly grubby Bar. "You don't look very surprised to see me," she complained.

"I'm still getting the dust out of my eyes."

Felice looked about her. "You haven't much luggage with you." She tittered provocatively. "I was hoping you'd be camping out and leaving Jonathan to have some time with me. I can't keep on staying with the Allans."

Bar winced. "What Jonathan does is nothing to do with me," she said stoically.

"My dear, I know that! But you are still living in his house, aren't you?"

"My house."

Felice raised disbelieving eyebrows. "Have it your own way—for now. I shan't have any difficulty getting rid of you when I'm ready to move in. I didn't like your father either. Jonathan gave him far too much of his own way for my liking, but he won't be making that mistake with you, I'll see to that."

Bar moved away towards the waiting Maasai, but her day was ruined by Felice's presence. When she shut her eyes, she could see Felice's fair head leaning against Jonathan's shoulder in her imagination. She burned with some new emotion she belatedly recognised as jealousy. What did it matter if she didn't like Felice? It was obvious that the other girl had a lot to offer. Felice might not speak Maa but she probably spoke the language of love.

It was one of the longest days Bar ever remembered. The sun beat down on the back of her head, grinding down her will power to stay in the saddle and prove to Jonathan that she knew what it was to work. She wouldn't have minded if either Michael or Felice had brought themselves to do anything useful, but the two of them just sat in the Cessna's shade, drinking a bottle of champagne that Michael brought with him and exchanging gossip about the friends they had in common in Nairobi, people whom Bar couldn't remember, even if she had ever known them.

Jonathan knew them all. Occasionally, he would join in with a comment while they were eating their picnic lunch, but mostly he was as silent as Bar. Once he looked up and caught her staring at him, and she knew he was very well aware that she was contrasting his actions with Michael's laziness and that the comparison was an irritant to her. She wanted to prefer Michael, but she didn't. The truth of the matter, she decided, was that Michael was proving to be as boring and out of place on the African plain as was the glamorous Felice.

"Tired?" Jonathan asked her.

She shook her head, but she wasn't being truthful. It was a long time since she had spent a whole day in the saddle, and she was sore and stiff, especially now that her muscles had tightened up during the picnic break.

"I'd rather get back to work," she answered him. "We'll never get done at this rate."

He touched her dusty cheek with a gentle hand. "Why don't you go back with the others? Someone else can bring your horse home."

Bar gritted her teeth. "I came to work, not to float round the skies when the going gets hard!"

Jonathan's eyebrows rose. "Okay, sweetheart, let's get on with it!"

Bar swallowed down the last of her piece of chicken, refusing Michael's half-hearted offer of

another glass of wine. She couldn't understand what
he was trying to do. The whole tone of the picnic was
misjudged in her view. This was meant to be a
working day, not a social occasion for eating and
frolicking! She got slowly to her feet, frowning into
the distance, where the Maasai were waiting with the
cattle.

"I did warn you," Jonathan murmured.

Bar gave him a speaking look. "She's your girl
friend!"

He grinned. "Jealous?"

"You're welcome to her!" Bar snapped.

But her heart was heavy as she rode away to take
up her station on the far side of the herd. Did
Jonathan, too, wish she would stay away from the
house tonight? She would be welcome at the Allans'
place, she knew, but now, more than ever, she
preferred to avoid it. It would encourage Michael to
think she might throw in her hand altogether. She
could imagine how eagerly he would put a call
through to her mother, and she had no intention of
going back to England, even if Jonathan succeeded
in throwing her bodily off her father's farm.

She thought the Allans had understood that she
was serious about the farm, but now she wondered.
If it had been Mrs. Allan's idea to pack up such a
lunch for them, she must have thought Bar was only
playing at working the cattle—as Michael would, as
Felice did.

The sun was setting when they rode home to the
farmhouse that evening. The Maasai had agreed to
guard their own herd as well as Jonathan's for the
night. They had seen the light aeroplane come and
go with a remarkable lack of interest. They them-

selves had gone the whole day without a break for food. Bar wondered what they thought of Michael's acrobatics in the air when he and Felice finally departed.

The farm workers drifted off, making their way to their own quarters. Most of them came from other tribes and were cautious in their dealings with the Maasai at the best of times. But they had worked well together that day and would again tomorrow. Bar knew that that was Jonathan's doing. He had worked as hard as any of them and yet his authority had been paramount, making the most of his disparate work force. She wouldn't have dared to challenge him herself, not while they were working.

Bar could see someone was smoking on the verandah when they came up to the house. The little red light came and went each time the smoker drew on the cigarette. A visitor now was all she needed, she reflected gloomily. She had dreamed of bath and bed all afternoon, frustrated by the knowledge that they wouldn't finish the dipping in one day, as she had hoped. It would take all her courage to get back into the saddle and ride out again tomorrow.

She slid off her mount, her knees buckling beneath her, and allowed the waiting African to lead the horse away to the stables. Felice's voice came to greet her, followed by a vision of feminine loveliness clad in a frothy chiffon evening dress.

"I missed your party last night, so I came tonight instead! You don't mind, do you? I had a look round the kitchen and I've decided more or less what we'll eat. You mustn't mind my taking over. This house is practically my second home."

Bar hoisted herself up the steps onto the verandah. "Explain it to Jonathan," she muttered. She threw herself into the nearest chair and groaned.

Felice fluttered with laughter, but Bar could tell she wasn't at all amused. "You never take any advice, do you? You've had Jonathan's attention all day. It's my turn now. Go to bed, Barbara Nelson, and keep out of my way. I've told Solomon to take your dinner to your room."

Bar wondered if she could find enough spirit to rebel. Every muscle ached and the thought of going to bed was an attractive one. If Jonathan wanted to entertain Felice, who was she to object?

Jonathan came striding up the steps and kissed Felice lightly on the cheek. "Did Michael come with you?" he asked.

Felice tucked her hand into his arm, looking up at him with soulful eyes. "I was stuck with him all day, darling. I came to be with you, so I had him drive me over and told him he could come back for me in the morning. We've both had a hard day in our own way. Surely we can please ourselves for one night?"

Jonathan looked down at Bar. "I don't think our hostess is up to it," he said.

Bar stirred uncomfortably. "Don't mind me!"

"We won't," Felice assured her in honeyed tones. She turned back to Jonathan. "Bar wants to go straight to bed. That's all right with us, isn't it?"

Bar could imagine the pleased delight on Jonathan's face. She refused to look at either of them. They were welcome to one another! She made a first attempt to get back on her feet, but nothing happened. The next moment Jonathan had yanked her upright and was guiding her inside the house and right into her bedroom.

"You never give in, do you?" he said. "Can you manage by yourself?"

Her eyes stung with tears. She must look a sight beside the elegant Felice. "Of course I can manage!" she almost shouted at him.

He put his fingers under her chin, raising her mouth to his. "If you shout, I'll come and help." His kiss was as gentle as a butterfly. Then he was gone, leaving her to her own devices.

It was a long time before Bar got off to sleep. She tried reading, turning the pages automatically, but what she was really doing was listening for Felice to go—or not go, which would be worse, because she couldn't bear to think of her spending the night with Jonathan.

In the middle of the night she was suddenly wide awake again, straining her ears in the silence. The African night was as black as velvet, scented with the smell of animals and growing things. She heard a lion's hunting cough and started out of her bed. Only her father's lioness would come so close to the house, especially if she were seeking food, and the baby gazelle would be a tempting morsel if the lioness knew her way in and out of the kitchen. Bar wondered if Solomon had shut the door properly when he left for his own quarters. Reluctantly she decided she would have to get up and see.

The gazelle was awake also, its nose twitching in distress at the noise outside. Bar would have wakened Jonathan on any other night but, if Felice was with him, he wouldn't relish being disturbed. She would have to cope by herself.

Bar tested all the doors and fastened the windows. The mosquito screens might not hold if the lioness should take it into her head to come in by the window.

"You're all right," she told the gazelle. "She can't possibly get in now."

If only she were half as certain as she sounded. Standing in the middle of the kitchen she could hear her own heartbeat. Everything else was silent. The lioness must have gone, though there was no telling when she would be back. She had had the run of the house most of her life and had no reason to be afraid of human beings. A shiver ran down Bar's spine. The creature might come in any time—there was no way they could keep up their guard night and day. Sooner or later, someone would forget to lock a window or a door and she would push her way in, as she must have done a hundred times before.

Bar hardly slept the rest of the night. Towards dawn, she drifted into a half-sleep from which she wakened, dry-eyed. Her muscles protested as she turned over. She must have been more frightened in the night than she had thought, for she had forgotten all about her aches and pains when she heard the lion's cough outside.

There was a sharp knock at the door. *"Karibu!"* she called out, and Solomon's head appeared, his eyes as large as saucers.

"Tikipit is here, *mama*. He wants to speak with Bwana Jonathan."

Bar groaned. "Why tell me?" she asked.

Then she remembered and started from the bed. "I suppose Memsahib Felice is still here?"

Solomon was noncommittal, but he had no intention of knocking on Jonathan's door. "I told Tikipit you would see him."

"I'm coming," Bar said. "Ask him into the kitchen, will you?"

She threw on some clothes, without bothering to do more than drag an impatient comb through her hair.

The Maasai was waiting outside the back door. His shaved head was decorated still in the ochre paint he had worn for his wedding day. Instead of a spear, he carried a lengthy stick with a knob at one end, and his dress was no more than a single cloth knotted over one shoulder.

Bar greeted him in Maa and he answered her gravely in the same tongue, changing suddenly to English. Somehow, she had forgotten that Tikipit was a university graduate, for a more unlikely one she had never seen. There was no changing the Maasai, she reflected, amused. Even when they met the white man on his own terms, they remained superior and remote, convinced their own ways were the only way for a real man to live.

"This is not for you, *mama*. I spoke to your man yesterday, and once before, about hunting down your father's lioness before she tastes human flesh again. The time has come. She has returned to the neighbourhood."

"I know," Bar said. "I heard her last night."

Tikipit nodded soberly. He was silent for a long moment, then he went on in his own tongue. "You were right to be frightened, but your man is the best shot in all Kenya. He won't allow you to be harmed. Our children were frightened too."

But not the men. It was all right for women and children to show fear and to huddle together for comfort, but men were made of sterner stuff. She shivered, remembering her fright in the night. Jonathan and Tikipit might not be frightened, but Michael would have been.

Jonathan's hand descended on her shoulder. He had thrown a dressing gown on, but it was obvious that he had nothing on underneath it. Bar felt herself blushing and turned away. A burning anger came up the back of her throat at the sight of him. Didn't he care that Felice was still a married woman? Nor had he any right to make Bar so aware of him as a man, just as though she were accustomed to having men walk round the house half-naked and unshaved! Did it take him long to shave? Her father, she remembered, had used a straight razor, but she thought Jonathan might prefer a more modern method.

Ashamed of her thoughts, she listened to the two men making arrangements for the lion hunt.

"Michael will go with you," she called out.

There was a moment's silence. "I'd as soon take you!" Jonathan answered. "Sooner, in fact!"

"I was coming anyway," she told him.

He came into the kitchen, tightening the cord of his dressing gown as he came. "You don't have to prove to me you're ready to tackle anything," he said. "I'm convinced of that already. It'll only hurt you to see your father's pet put down, and we have no choice, Bar. She could kill again any time. You'd never forgive yourself if she took a Maasai child—as she nearly did last night."

Bar clenched her fists. "That's why I have to come. I have to finish what my father began. Can't you see that?"

Jonathan looked at her for a long moment, his face

expressionless. "Your boyfriend will expect us to apply for a licence, but there's no time for that."

"No," she agreed. "We don't have to tell him anything about it, do we? Unless Felice—"

Jonathan grinned at her. "You can safely leave Felice to me," he said.

Chapter Ten

There was no sign of Felice anywhere in the house when Bar checked her father's guns, choosing the smaller of the two rifles for her own use. She wondered how Jonathan had persuaded her to go.

"When are we leaving?" she asked Jonathan when he paused in his own preparations to check on hers.

"After dark tonight."

That late? Bar wondered if she would be able to stay awake through the hours of daylight. She agreed that something had to be done about the lioness— and she was prepared to do it. But all those hours in which to think about it! She would start thinking of what the lioness had meant to her father, of how she should have been beside him, how she might have persuaded him to train the animal to go back to the wild and live among her own kind, of how important it was for a lion to be a lion and not a make-believe human being. She'd think of all that and when it came time to go and hunt her father's pet down in cold blood, she wouldn't be able to do it.

The radio-telephone crackled in the corner of the office and she realised belatedly that Jonathan had been talking to someone when she came in. Was it Felice?

But it was Peter Allan's voice that spoke into the silence, scratchy and unlike himself, but not at all like Felice's well-modulated tones.

"You can't go by yourself, Jonathan. We'll all come."

Jonathan spoke into the microphone. "Come by yourself, Peter."

"Michael's a good shot. Over."

"I don't want him. Over."

"Okay, I'll do my best. Meet you at the top at seven-thirty anyway. Over and out."

The instrument went dead, responding to the flick of Jonathan's finger. "Peter should know better!" was all he said.

"Michael is a good shot," Bar insisted.

"You'd think so whether he was or not," Jonathan replied. "Personally, I'd prefer to have him on the other side. Less chance of being shot in the back that way."

"Jonathan!"

"Saving your presence and all that. I'd forgotten he's a friend of yours."

Bar knew he hadn't forgotten anything. She puzzled over the incident for most of the morning. Was it possible that Felice was double-dealing with Michael behind Jonathan's back? It seemed unlikely, but one couldn't tell with Felice.

Bar decided not to argue when Jonathan told her to stay round the house all day. She made a token protest about doing her share and riding out to see how they were managing later on, but they both knew she had no intention of making the long ride out across the plains by herself. Jonathan wouldn't have gone either, except that they couldn't keep the herd penned up in one small area for long. They would run out of feed long before they finished at that rate.

Bar checked on her gazelle more times than she cared to count during the day. When she wasn't doing that, she sat around thinking about her future on the farm. If the Allans were mortgaged to the hilt, who held the deed on their place? There was only one answer to that. She knew it as clearly as night followed day. Jonathan did.

He looked tired when he came home that evening. He was certainly irritable. He scarcely said two words while they ate their evening meal. Nor did Bar have much to say. If she'd said anything at all, she would be tempted to plead with him to send Felice back to Nairobi, because she was no good for him and never would be. And how did you tell a fully grown man that? Felice wasn't right for him! Felice would bore him silly before the honeymoon was over. But she couldn't tell him that.

Jonathan brought his Landrover round the foot of the verandah steps.

"Sure you want to go?" he asked her as she got in beside him, resting her broken rifle across her knees.

"I must go," she said.

His eyes rested briefly on her set face. "Can't you trust me to do the job for you?"

Her hands tightened on the rifle until her knuckles showed white. Without any change of expression, Jonathan took it from her and put it on the back seat with his own.

"Nobody'll think any the worse of you if you stay home," he went on casually.

"I would," she said. "It was my father who set this up by his stupidity, and I have a responsibility towards the farm—and the Maasai—just because I'm his daughter."

"The farm is my responsibility, not yours," he contradicted her.

Bar shook her head. "I'm the only Nelson here," she said.

Jonathan shrugged. "Okay, have it your own way, but the Nelsons haven't had any say around here for a long time now and the farm still goes on. Besides, you won't be a Nelson for ever. Have you thought of that?"

She threw him a mutinous look. "That's just the sort of male chauvinist thing I'd expect you to say!"

But he only laughed at her. "I believe in facing facts," he said. "Unfortunately the Nelsons don't—"

He drove off at top speed and she was forced to hang on to whatever she could in order to keep her seat. Since when had she not faced facts? She had never expected to get anything for nothing. True, she wanted her share of the farm, but she was prepared to work as hard as he did in return for the living she hoped it would give her. She was entitled to her father's share.

But suppose her father had sold out, as the Allans had? Bar couldn't believe the direction her thoughts were taking. Her father would never do anything of the sort! The farm had been his whole life, just as she intended it to be hers. Her father would never have sold out knowing that she was planning on joining him as soon as she was ready to do so, but had he understood that? Her mother never believed she really meant to return to Kenya. Had her father been assured that she wasn't coming?

"I worked so hard not to be a disappointment to him," she worried aloud. "He must have believed I was coming. I wrote him I was coming as soon as I got my degree."

"Your mother planned for you to stay in England," Jonathan put in.

"But *I* didn't!"

"Your father last saw you when you were twelve years old. You were a child to him until the day he died."

Bar sniffed. "He sold out to you, didn't he?" she accused him. "Why didn't you tell me? Why did you let me go on believing I had a right to be here?"

"You weren't doing me any harm. Your father was entitled to go on living here for as long as he wanted to—"

"I'm not my father!"

"No, you're not. You seemed to think you'd inherited his rights, though, and I thought you'd get tired of it at first."

"At first?"

"Later on, I realised you were a better farmer than your father ever was. Why should I disturb a good working partnership?"

"Felice—"

"I don't run my life to suit Felice, or anyone else.

Be quiet now, we're coming up to the meeting place. I want to get into position before there's any danger of frightening her off."

Bar did as she was told. The spirit had gone out of her for the moment and she was very conscious that she was here as Jonathan's guest. She had no rights in anything to do with the farm after all.

There was no moon that night. Bar could hardly see the faces of the people who had come to join in the hunt. She saw the Allans and Felice, looking strange and excited, and Tikipit and his Maasai standing a short way off. They were all waiting for Jonathan to tell them what to do, she realised, and she was ashamed for them. They had lived on the same patch of land all their lives, and yet none of them was prepared to take any responsibility for what they were all about to do.

"If we can, we'll capture her and hand her over to the Wild Life Department alive," Jonathan ordered. "She sits up in a tree a little way from here when she isn't hunting. I've brought a net and a tranquillising dart, so please don't shoot unless you have to. Is that all clear?"

Felice giggled. "Lions don't sit in trees!" she said.

"That's all you know," Jonathan said. "In Tanzania, I've seen whole prides take to the trees."

"I'll believe it when I see it!" Felice cut him off. "You're too soft-hearted for your own good, Jonathan. She'll be better off dead. Are you sure Bar hasn't talked you into this silly rescue plan?"

"Bar didn't know about it." Jonathan's face was taut. "Shall we go?"

They took up their positions around the tree as

Jonathan indicated to them, Bar as far away from Felice as she could get. She wondered what had brought the other woman out at night on such a mission and concluded it was the excitement of bagging a lion.

She climbed an acacia tree to give herself a better view. From where she was sitting, she could see the yellow streaks on the branch where the lioness sometimes slept. Would she come there tonight? They might have a very long wait before them.

An hour later Bar thought she heard a movement in the thickets round the tree. She tensed her muscles and waited. The lioness might well smell the trap they had laid for her, for there was no wind to disguise their scent. She did pause for an instant, sniffing the air, but this lioness was accustomed to the smell of people and she was completely unafraid, unlike her genuinely wild peers. She leaped lightly onto a lower branch of her chosen tree and a rifle cracked into life, following a shrill female scream. The lioness turned and half fell to the ground. Bar saw her turn and face her attacker, saw Jonathan step out into the clearing, and she raised her own rifle, took aim and squeezed the trigger.

For a terrible instant she thought she had been too late. The lioness rose onto her back feet, ready to pounce, but at the critical moment she fell to the ground, dead.

Jonathan came over to Bar's tree, yanking her down from her branch as if she weighed no more than thistledown. "Didn't I tell you *not* to shoot unless I told you to? You've killed her!"

"She would have killed you otherwise," Bar wept.

"Not if you hadn't wounded her in the first place!"

"But I didn't!"

Jonathan shook her hard. Her hair fell loose down her back and the tears spurted from her eyes.

"I didn't! I didn't!" she shouted at him.

"You're nothing but a spoilt child!" he shouted back. He forced her across the rough ground, releasing her into Mrs. Allan's care. "Keep her out of my way while I see what can be done," he snapped out.

Alice Allan put a comforting arm about Bar's shoulders. "Never mind, dear. He'll get over it."

"I don't want him to get over it, the big bully!" Bar retorted. "Who fired that first shot?"

"Didn't you?"

"No, I did not!"

"Then why didn't you tell him so?"

Bar brushed twigs off her trousers. "He didn't give me any opportunity to say much." She managed a feeble smile, sniffing back her tears. "Oh well, I wasn't staying anyway. He doesn't want me here and I've decided to go quietly."

"Back to England?"

Bar sniffed again. It was a bleak prospect, but it was nothing to cry about, she told herself angrily. "I'll try Nairobi first," she said.

It was too dark to see what the men were doing. Or Felice. Bar hadn't given the other girl a thought since they had taken up their stations, but she remembered now that female scream and then the first crack of a rifle.

"Where's Felice?" she asked the older woman.

"Who cares?" Alice answered. "She's the most difficult guest I've ever had to deal with. I'd do anything for Jonathan, but either she comes in at a proper time or she stays away. Last night was the very last time that I'll sit up with her half the night, making cups of tea and listening to her tales of that husband of hers!"

"Last night?" Bar repeated.

But Alice was still following her own train of thought. "I don't believe she really wants to leave Luciano at all! Jonathan said so all along, but I didn't believe him."

"I'd better go and find her," Bar said.

"Leave her to Jonathan," Alice advised.

Bar dragged herself to her feet. Her knees shook, almost refusing to support her, and there was an ache in her chest.

"Are you sure you're all right?" Alice asked her anxiously.

"I hope so," Bar said.

She forced herself to walk the short distance back to the men, averting her eyes from the body of her father's pet lion. Jonathan had turned the animal over and was squatting down beside it, staring at the great gash the first bullet had ripped in her side. Peter Allan was beside him, and so was Tikipit, a more excited and voluble Tikipit than Bar had ever seen.

"The first bullet came from over there!" He gesticulated violently in the opposite direction from where Bar had been stationed.

"I told you—" Bar began shakily.

Tikipit nodded his head and went on in Maa, "He was anxious for you, nothing more. He wanted to keep the lion alive for you. Isn't that enough for you?"

Bar swallowed. Did everyone know she was in love with Jonathan?

"Would you have let her live?" she retorted.

"If my woman pleased me very much and wanted her alive," he answered indifferently. "Your man—"

"He isn't my man! Have you seen the other *memsahib?*"

"Not with my eyes."

Bar sighed. "Where is she?" she demanded.

Tikipit pointed into the darkness just as Jonathan rose to his feet. "What are you talking about?" he asked irritably.

"I'm worried about Felice," Bar confessed.

"Isn't she with Michael?"

Didn't he care? Bar took a deep breath as the pain in her chest magically vanished. "I don't know," she said.

She began walking in the direction Tikipit had pointed out to her. It was darker still in amongst the trees and her breath caught in her throat when she heard a footstep close behind her. Her relief when she saw it was Jonathan was correspondingly great.

"What makes you think I'm not your man?" he asked her pleasantly.

Bar missed her footing and would have fallen if Jonathan hadn't caught her. "Well?" he insisted.

Her eyes opened wide. "You understand Maa!" she accused him.

"A little."

"Then why pretend you don't?"

"I don't speak it like a native," he teased her. "It was your proof that you belonged here."

"Much good it did me. I don't belong here!"

"I thought you were a Nelson?"

Her depression returned and with it her tiredness. "The Nelsons sold out long ago. I didn't know it, that's all."

Felice was crouched at the foot of a tree, her rifle flung away in a bush not far away. She was crying hysterically to herself, all thoughts of her appearance gone for the moment. "I could have been killed!" she moaned, over and over again. "Michael said it would be fun, but I hated it all. I could have been killed, and nobody would have even cared! I want Luciano!"

"Of course you do," Jonathan agreed in bracing tones.

"We could all have been killed!"

"I might have been if Bar hadn't kept her head."

Felice clung to him, burying her face in his shoulder. "I saw her! Did you see her? I kept thinking how she killed Bob Nelson! None of us were safe while she was still alive—so I called out! Did you hear me call out, Jonathan? Why didn't you shoot her dead then?"

"I didn't know she'd been wounded. Did you try to shoot her?"

Felice shuddered. "Me? I couldn't kill anything! You know that! I was terribly frightened—"

Jonathan pushed her away and retrieved her rifle from the bush, sniffing the barrel suspiciously. "Who fired that first shot?" he demanded.

Felice uttered a small scream, only too glad to tell him. "Michael did! Michael was as frightened as I was!"

"It figures," Jonathan said in disgust.

"Where is Michael?" Bar asked.

"He ran away. He left me here all alone. I'll

never, never spend another night like this one, I can tell you! I'm going back to Nairobi with Michael tomorrow and then I'm going to take the first plane down to the coast. Luciano wouldn't expect me to go through an ordeal like this! He knows how to look after a woman!"

"He always did," Jonathan reminded her.

He helped Felice back to the vehicles, almost carrying her part of the way, leaving Bar to follow as and when she would. There was no doubt which of them could capture and keep his attention, Bar thought dolefully. No doubt by morning he would have persuaded her to change her mind and to think of the evening as a great adventure. The sooner Bar took herself off to Nairobi the better, she decided. Jonathan had made it quite clear that he didn't want her around.

The Allans were waiting in their Landrover. Michael pointedly looked the other way as Jonathan helped Felice into the front seat. Bar looked at his grim expression and put out an anxious hand.

"Would you rather Felice went with you?" she began breathlessly.

He blocked her approach to the Landrover by the simple expedient of placing his body in her way. "Don't you dare!" he growled at her.

She fell back, defeated. What did he want? she wondered.

Peter Allan started up the Landrover and let in the clutch, driving slowly away over the rough ground, until only the red of the rear lights could be seen, and then nothing remained but the distant hum of the engine.

Bar felt Jonathan's hand slip round her waist and

resisted the temptation to lean back against him as she wanted to do.

"You have more clothes on this evening," he said in her ear. "Pity."

"It's cold out after dark."

"Is that why you're shivering?"

Bar made a movement away from him, but he pulled her back against him. "I'm sorry it had to be you who killed her," he said.

Bar squared her shoulders. "She would have killed you otherwise. I wasn't going to have that on my conscience as well as everything else!"

"What else?"

"I should have been here!" she declared passionately. "My father should have known better than to keep a lion round the house, but it was my fault too. I thought we belonged here and we don't."

Jonathan stiffened. "What makes you say that?"

"I haven't any claim on the farm."

"I'm not sending you away," he said.

"No, you're not," she answered proudly. "I'm going of my own free will."

She pulled away from him and climbed into the Landrover, returning her rifle to the back seat. It had shocked her to see how both Michael and Felice could use dangerous firearms as if they mattered not a jot to either of them. Michael, at least, should have known better. She was glad she had never paid much attention to her mother's lavish praise of him. She had liked Michael, but she would always be a stranger to him. Jonathan would never have fired in panic. Jonathan knew the land as well as she did—better. It was as if the life she had always loved had depended on Jonathan from the very beginning.

Without him, it was dust and ashes and as unreward-ing as the life her mother wanted her to lead in England.

When they reached the house, she jumped out of the Landrover and went straight to her room. She sat down in front of the dressing table and looked at herself in the glass. She looked a mess, with the trace of tears still on her cheeks and her hair, full of twigs and dead leaves, flying in a knotted mass round her head. She picked up her brush and began to brush her hair as if her life depended on it. And at that moment the lights went out.

"Did you forget to prime the generator?"

She could feel Jonathan's presence in her room and she was afraid. "Go away!"

"I want to talk to you."

"There's nothing to talk about!"

"Isn't there?" His hands clamped down on her shoulders and he turned her round to face him. "We have this much to talk about. You want to be here and I want you here. I want you!"

"Only because Felice—"

His lips met hers in a hard kiss. "If you can't say something sensible, you'd better shut up!" And he kissed her again.

Her arms went up round his neck without con-scious volition. The feel of him was exciting, making her come alive again. It was dangerous being so close to him, but it was a sweet danger.

"Any woman would do!" she protested, hoping he would brush away the objection by telling her she was the one and only woman for him.

"Any woman isn't here."

She could have cried with disappointment. "I'm

going to Nairobi in the morning and then I won't be here either!"

His hands slipped under her shirt and came up against the barrier of her brassiere. She pulled away from him before he could find the clasp.

"You're here now," he said quietly.

She caught her lower lip between her teeth. "That's all you've ever thought of me, isn't it? Someone on the lookout for a man because she can't live without one! But that isn't me! I wanted Africa, not a man, not you, not anyone!"

His arms tightened about her and she could no longer force herself to reject him. What nonsense she was talking! He was everything she had ever wanted from the first moment she had set eyes on him! Why pretend otherwise?

"We'll talk about it in the morning," he said, a thread of laughter running under the words.

"We won't!"

His kiss made her ache with longing for him. Her body arched against his and her response was as passionate and as inevitable as the sea throwing itself against a rocky shore in a storm.

"Good night, my love," he said against her ear, and then he was gone, slamming her bedroom door behind him.

Left alone, Bar cried bitterly. If he had wanted her, he would have taken her, she reasoned. There was nothing left for her in life but loneliness and exile. She had thought her home was Africa, but it wasn't. The only home she would ever want was in Jonathan's arms.

Chapter Eleven

Bar was in the office, finishing off the government forms that were due, when Jonathan came across from the house, whistling under his breath.

"Where have you been?" she asked him crossly. "You knew I was going to Nairobi today."

"I thought you might change your mind," he answered cheerfully.

She could have strangled him there and then. "Why should I?" she demanded.

"It's a long way to go on your own."

She remembered how far it had seemed when she had been coming the other way. She remembered, too, the end of that long drive, and the colour came into her cheeks. He had kissed her several times since then, but that had been the first time she ever felt an overwhelming response for any man. Why did it have to be Jonathan?

She eyed him across the desk, noting how wide his shoulders were beneath his short-sleeved shirt and how his hair had grown since she had first seen him. He badly needed a haircut. She wondered what he would say if she offered to give him one as a parting present. One never knew with Jonathan. He might just take her up on the offer.

"I might fly up to Nairobi with Michael," she murmured, not meaning a word of it.

Jonathan sat on the edge of her desk. "Too late! I've just got back from seeing the two of them off, both Michael and Felice. Neither of them will be back in a hurry."

Bar looked down at her hands, deliberately hiding her eyes from him. She hadn't slept well and the sight of Jonathan, sitting there, very much at his ease, struck her as unfair, while she felt as though she were riding an emotional scenic railway. Why couldn't he ever get all worked up instead of looking as though he had the whole world on a string?

"Will they report the death of the lion?"

"Nope. I put a call in to Nairobi first thing this morning and told them all about it. There'll be some more forms for you to fill in coming through the post."

"I won't be here!"

He leaned towards her. "Want to bet on that?"

"I have no business being here, now that I know the farm is all yours. I thought it was what I wanted. I worked very hard to be of use here, but you don't need or want me here—"

"Supposing I ask you to stay?"

"I can't!" The words burst out of her. "Don't you see that I can't?" she added on a whisper.

"Why can't you?"

She licked her lips. It was a provocative gesture, but she was completely unaware of it. She had other things on her mind.

"Because—"

"Yes?" he prompted her.

She looked up suddenly, her eyes dark with purpose. "Because I may fight you over the ownership of the farm even yet. In Nairobi I can get a solicitor to look over the papers. My father must have retained some rights for himself. He went on living here."

"I'm not averse to your living here!" he protested.

"On your terms, or mine?"

He smiled. "What are your terms?" he asked.

She took a deep breath. "Fifty-fifty?"

"Your Maasai friends would never agree to that."

"I'm not a Maasai."

He looked thoughtfully at her. "I wonder if we're talking about the same thing," he said at last.

She was struck dumb. Surely he didn't expect her to make all the running? It was dangerous ground she was treading on. It had taken her the whole night to come as far as she had, spurred on by Felice's declaration that she was going back to her husband. But she couldn't do it all by herself! Jonathan had to tell her what he wanted too—and it was more than possible that it didn't include her.

"A partnership?" he suggested, coming closer still.

"What kind of a partnership?"

If he really had been out to see Michael and Felice off, he had taken the time to shower and change his clothes since he got back. She could smell the remnants of the shampoo on his hair and the smell of his newly ironed clothes. She refused to look at him, sure that he must be able to hear her heart pounding against her ribs.

"Humph," he said. "How about bed and board with the possibility of progressing to complete joint ownership?"

Her skin prickled. "What would you want in exchange?" Her voice had deserted her and the words came out in a squeak. As she cleared her throat she brushed against him and a wave of delight spread through her.

"You," he said.

She really looked at him then. Her whole being was filled with his essence and she clutched at him to steady herself.

"I thought you wanted Felice?"

Jonathan's hands slipped beneath her elbows, lifting her up towards him and the lips that would plunder hers if she didn't turn her face away. She couldn't move at all.

"Luciano Arghetti is a friend of mine. I was best man at his wedding."

"Mrs. Allan thought you were going to marry Felice!"

"She had no reason to do so. It may have crossed Felice's mind, but only as a stick to beat Luciano with."

"You didn't seem reluctant to have her come down here and visit you," Bar disapproved.

Jonathan grinned at her. "A best man should do his best to keep in touch with the husband's interests, don't you think?"

She raised her brows. "Such a close interest?"

"Why not? A brush with the romance of Africa was quite enough to send her scurrying back to Luciano. Not everyone can cope with Africa in the raw—or me either!"

The colour came rushing into Bar's face. "How did you get that scar?"

His voice was so deep that it was like listening to the sea moving over gravel. It was a sound guaranteed to undermine her defences and she loved every minute of it.

"I was a very young man in those days. Bar, if I were to kiss you now, would you whip off your sandal and lay my face open?"

She shook her head. "Who was she?"

His eyes were dark and she could see her own reflection deep within them. It was where she always wanted to be. She blinked, disturbed by the gnawing anxiety inside her that he might have loved—really loved—the girl in question.

"Jealous?" he asked.

There was a complacent note to his voice that reassured her.

"Yes," she said. "Silly, isn't it?"

"Very silly."

Silly or not, she couldn't resist questioning him further. "Was she an Arab? Arab women defend themselves that way, don't they?"

"No, she wasn't an Arab. She married someone else—someone with better prospects at the time, or so she thought."

"She was a fool," Bar said very softly.

His lips brushed against hers. "Tikipit tells me his mother thinks you a wise woman. Are we partners?"

She badly wanted him to kiss her properly, to take

her into his arms and hold her until her doubts
vanished.

"I don't know," she said foolishly.

His fingers trailed across her cheek, pressing her
lips apart with his thumb, before he kissed her again
and she tasted his tongue against hers and thought
she might faint with the pleasure of it. What did it
matter why he wanted her to stay? She would never
find the strength to leave him now.

"There'll never be any other woman for me,
Barbara Nelson. Give in to the inevitable and stay
here with me. If you're afraid of the loneliness, we'll
move in closer to Nairobi. Only I can't let you go! I
know now how your father felt when you and your
mother left him for England. If I had to, I'd follow
you there, but I think we'd both be happier somewhere in this country."

"Oh, Jonathan!" she exclaimed. "I don't care
where we live, I only want to be with you!"

"As my wife?"

She flung her arms round his neck. "I lied to you
last night," she confessed. "I wanted you to stay
with me. I've wanted you to make love to me ever
since you first kissed me. It was awful thinking I
didn't mean anything to you!"

His arms closed round her in a most satisfactory
way. "A wise woman!" he mocked. "How many
times do I have to tell you I want you?"

She hid her face in his neck. "In passing. I thought
you wanted Felice for keeps. Even last night, I still
thought I was second best. If I were, though, you
wouldn't marry me, would you?"

"Second best doesn't last."

She turned her face up to his. "I know, but you'll never be second best for me. I love you very much."

She was amused by the startled expression on his face. "You do?"

"Very much!" she confirmed.

"Good," he said, "because I love you too."

"How are we going to get to Nairobi?" she asked.

"We're going to fly up in Peter's plane."

"Can you pilot the thing?"

"I can. It'd take far too long to drive. They'll only marry us if we can get there before three o'clock."

"I have to change! I can't go dressed like this!"

"I wouldn't care if you came in your birthday suit," he told her, watching the emotions play over her face.

She pretended to be shocked. "I soon will be in my birthday suit if you go on like that!" she rebuked him.

"I can't wait!"

He held her closer against him, keeping her there with strong thighs locked against hers. He smiled deep into her eyes, kissing the tip of her nose. "How about getting married tomorrow?" he suggested.

"Tomorrow never comes," she replied promptly.

"Does it matter?"

The laughter fell away from her face. "It matters to me. I want to be yours in every way, not just—"

"I know, love."

The touch of his hands against her bare back was oddly reassuring. She leaned against him, searching her mind for the words to tell him why it mattered to her that she should have his ring on her finger before she shared his bed.

She found his shirt beneath her fingers, and pleated it, smoothing it out again with a fierce concentration and knowing that he was watching her, waiting for her to say what was in her mind.

"I've never given myself to anyone before," she said unsteadily. "When I do, I want it to consummate our marriage, to make it permanent, because it means everything to me. Does that make sense?"

"Yes, darling, I think it does. What I have, I hold—for ever. If you need to be married to me before you can be sure of that, it's okay with me."

She pleated the shirt again. "Perhaps it was the way I was brought up, but I want everything to be right for both of us."

"And so it shall be."

But at the touch of his hands on her breasts, coupled with his long passionate kisses, she wondered if it was, after all, really worthwhile. If he wanted to bed her before he married her, why should she care? Was she so impossibly respectable that she had to have a licence made out in their names before she could allow him to make her his own?

"I wish we didn't have to go," she said in broken tones.

"Because you want me?" he tempted her, nibbling at her ear.

"More than life itself!"

He swung her away from him. "Then go and get changed, woman, and let's get going."

Bar felt unexpectedly self-conscious as she sat beside Jonathan in his Landrover, dressed in a silk dress and a hat to match. She had enjoyed the wedding ceremony and she had enjoyed the meal Jonathan had treated her to afterwards. She had enjoyed her brief stay in the sophisticated atmosphere of Nairobi, and she had felt quite right there. It was only now, when they were alone with nothing but the plains of Africa all around them, that she had started to feel out of place and more than a little nervous about what Jonathan might expect of her.

He seemed a stranger, someone she didn't know at all, and she couldn't help worrying whether he had really wanted to marry her. Wouldn't he have been happier if they had just gone on as they had before?

"Want to go home by way of the escarpment?" Jonathan asked her, slanting a glance at her that made her look away and did something peculiar to her breathing.

She nodded her head. What did it matter which way they went? It was the getting-home bit that bothered her. He had been charming and distant all the time they had been in Nairobi, but what would it be like to be alone with him at home as his wife?

He drew up at the spot where they had first met, parking the Landrover neatly out of the sun. Then he turned towards her, holding out his hands to her.

"What's the matter, Bar?" he asked her.

"I don't know," she said. "I was wondering—"

"Yes?"

It was impossible to explain her doubts to him. She couldn't even explain them to herself. She sat, picking at her cotton gloves, until he took them away from her and threw them onto the back seat.

"Am I right in thinking this is rather a special place to you?"

She licked her lips nervously. "In a way," she admitted.

"Tell me about it," he invited her.

That was easier said than done. "I used to ride out here as a child," she began. "Towards the end I used to come often. It wasn't much fun at home just then."

Funny how long it was since she had thought about that. She had taught herself to forget the endless arguments and the wild accusations her parents had flung at one another. Her mother would go on a visit to Nairobi and it would always be the same on her return. Her father had been a jealous, possessive man, and perhaps he had had cause. Her mother had been bored stiff by everything to do with the life he lived.

"I know what you did in Nairobi," Jonathan said gently. "You married me, remember?"

That brought another memory to mind, a more recent one, when she had stopped here on her way to her father's house.

"When you found me here it was the day of Tikipit's wedding. I watched him taking his bride home to his compound. He went striding on ahead and she followed behind looking scared stiff. Tikipit's friend helped her over the rough patches, but Tikipit never even glanced her way. I wondered if all brides felt the same way, leaving their old life behind and going with some man to a strange place amongst strange people. She was little more than a child."

"How do you feel?" Jonathan asked.

She brushed the question aside. "I shall be living in the house of my childhood. It's different for me."

"Is it?"

No, she longed to tell him, it wasn't different at all. He was a stranger to her and she didn't know what he would expect of her. In one way the Maasai girl had been lucky. She had known every detail of what her life would be like, even though it would be strange to her. She knew she would be welcomed by her mother-in-law who would expect her to obey her every word. She knew that Tikipit would review his cattle and choose the best of them for her to look after, their progeny eventually going to her children when they were old enough. She knew that he would count all her children as his, though after the first children he might not be the father of them all.

"I've never wanted to live anywhere else," she said aloud, "but I thought it was mine then. Now I have to remember it's yours."

He looked straight ahead of him across the plains below. "Is that why you married me?"

Was it? Could she say it had nothing to do with it?

"My parents always had a row when they got back from Nairobi," she said, apropos of nothing at all.

Jonathan relaxed visibly. "We're going to make love," he said, "just as soon as I get you home."

"I'm afraid that we'll have rows too," she murmured.

"I know you are."

She was startled. "How can you know that?"

He turned her face to his. "I lived with your father for quite a few years. I know what he was like, sweetheart, and whilst we got along very well together, I'm nothing like him."

"Aren't you?"

The finely chiselled mouth straightened, looking stern. "You'll find it difficult to have a row with me. We'll make love instead."

"You may not always want to," she objected.

He forced her chin up. "That's what you think!" His expression softened. "You won't be going to Nairobi by yourself. I need you beside me, to warm my heart by just looking at you, and to have you there to love and to love me. You won't have time to be going off places by yourself."

Her lips trembled into a smile and she shut her eyes in relief.

"I love you," she said.

He kissed her softly on the lips. "It won't always be easy," he warned her. "I'm used to being on my own. I thought it was what I wanted, until I met you. I knew I couldn't let you go. I wanted you then and I want you now. I'll never be complete away from you again. If that's loving you, my darling, then I love you very much. I'm empty without you."

"Is that why you didn't tell me about buying my father out?"

"I wanted you in the house. At first I thought I'd talk you into my bed and, after a while, the feeling would wear off, but then I started wondering what it would be like after you'd gone. The wedding ceremony was for you, my sweet. You've been the wife of my heart for many days now, and you always will be."

Bar knew contentment mixed with a growing excitement that she had never felt before. This time there would be no breaking off, no going back, this time Jonathan would take her all the way to the top.

"I'm ready to go home," she said.

The house was deserted when they walked together up the steps to the verandah.

"Do you want something to eat?" Bar asked.

"I'm more hungry for you."

She blushed, rather shy of this large, comforting husband of hers. "You'll have to wait," she told him. "I left my room in a mess—"

"You're sharing mine from now on!"

"Am I?" She had never slept in any bedroom but the one she had as a child in this house. "I'll still need to move my things. I think I'll have a bath."

"Have a shower and I'll join you!"

She considered him, relishing each and every detail of his appearance. He was strong physically, she had always known that, but he was strong mentally too, she thought. It occurred to her that neither of her parents had shown much inclination for facing up to facts. That had largely been the trouble in their marriage. Jonathan was right, it would be different for them, not because of anything she did, but because she could trust him to deal with every event of life as it came along. Jonathan was no Michael to be managed and flattered, he was a man, and she hugged the knowledge to her, disbelieving her own luck at becoming his bride.

Her lips curved into a smile. "Will you wash my back?"

His eyes glinted. "If you'll wash mine."

She had never had a shower with anyone before. For a long time she couldn't bring herself to do anything except stand outside the curtain with a towel wound round her. If she thought Jonathan would have any truck with his bride's modesty, she was wrong. He drew the curtains back with a flourish, taking the towel from her and throwing it deep into the room.

"You're beautiful, Bar," he told her, allowing his eyes to run over her from the top of her pinned-back hair to her sunburned toes. "I knew you were the first time I saw you, but you're even more beautiful than I had imagined."

She turned away from him. She wanted to look at him too, but she could see nothing but her own embarrassment. She hugged her arms across her breasts and stepped under the water. His arms reached out to receive her, pulling her close against him. He was very wet and his body hair was rough against the silkiness of her skin. She cast him an anxious look as his toes stepped on hers, but he ignored her bashfulness, picking up the soap and solemnly beginning to apply it, soaping her back, her breasts, down her waist and across her flat stomach. Then he passed the soap to her.

"Your turn," he said.

It took her much longer to get a satisfactory foam on his broad shoulders and across his well-muscled chest.

Jonathan reached up and turned off the shower. He stepped out and retrieved her towel, wrapping her in it as he would a child. She made a small effort to dry herself, turning her back on him. She was quite unprepared for his exuberant yell as he lifted

her bodily against his chest and carried her down the
corridor to his bed.

Tikipit's bride served them all with the honey beer
the Maasai men are so fond of. Bar refused her
share, a smile playing on her lips as she watched
Jonathan take a good swig straight from the gourd in
which it was kept. How had she ever thought he was
out of place here? she wondered.

"So you stay amongst us?" Tikipit's mother commented. "It was what your father wanted for you."

"I hope so," Bar agreed.

"He would be glad to see your sons growing on
your land." She laughed the earthy laugh of women
close to the elements everywhere. "Your man will
enjoy getting them! It's good when a man's pleasure
and a woman's are one."

Bar expelled her breath in a noncommittal sound
that said nothing.

"You are growing vegetables," the old woman
said suddenly.

"Yes, I am."

"I have heard. It used to be said it was an evil to
break the crust of the earth and to sow seeds, but the
land won't allow us always to herd our cattle in
freedom under the sky." She put out a hard, boney
hand. "Do always as your man bids you and you'll
come to no harm. He is one of us."

Bar grinned. "He doesn't speak Maa!"

"He speaks to the heart. He'll understand well
enough all that you have to say to him."

"Yes, he does," Bar admitted with a calm she was
far from feeling. "I am glad to be his woman."

The old woman cackled with laughter. "I've made

you a collar of beads for your marriage. Shall I put it on for you, or will your man?"

"I will," Jonathan interrupted firmly. He took the wide collar from Tikipit's mother, examining with interest the thousands of tiny beads arranged in a traditional pattern of many collars with interest. "You must tell me what it means?"

But none of the Maasai would tell him. They hinted at many things, that the sky god they worshipped was pleased by the marriage, but the stories they told became more and more obscure until they were meaningless to anyone but themselves.

Only as Jonathan and Bar were preparing to go did Tikipit touch Jonathan lightly on the arm. "The Maasai are your brothers, that's the true meaning," he said.

Bar whispered a thankyou, her heart leaping at Jonathan's touch as he placed the collar about her neck. Both woman laughed to themselves at her reaction, the older one poking her in the ribs.

"He's in a hurry to take you home!" she teased her.

It was Jonathan who answered her, a broad grin on his face, answering her in her own language with a facility that left Bar breathless and very proud of him.

"When one's happiness rests in such a woman, one is always in a hurry to take her home!"

And he bent his head and kissed her on the lips as a promise of what was to come. She kissed him back, still smiling.

"I love you, Jonathan Grant!" she told him.

"Then come home and prove it," he commanded.

She went, without a single backward look, her hand in his. It was for this that she had been born, to stand beside Jonathan on their own land, welding together the past and the future of their small part of the continent of Africa.

15-Day Free Trial Offer
6 Silhouette Romances

6 Silhouette Romances, free for 15 days! We'll send you 6 new Silhouette Romances to keep for 15 days, absolutely free! If you decide not to keep them, send them back to us. You pay nothing.

Free Home Delivery. But if you enjoy them as much as we think you will, keep them by paying the invoice enclosed with your free trial shipment. We'll pay all shipping and handling charges. You get the convenience of Home Delivery and we pay the postage and handling charge each month.

Don't miss a copy. The Silhouette Book Club is the way to make sure you'll be able to receive every new romance we publish before they're sold out. There is no minimum number of books to buy and you can cancel at any time.

This offer expires April 30, 1984

Silhouette Book Club, Dept. **SRSR7D**
120 Brighton Road, Clifton, NJ 07012

Please send me 6 Silhouette Romances to keep for 15 days, absolutely free. I understand I am not obligated to join the Silhouette Book Club unless I decide to keep them.

NAME_____

ADDRESS_____

CITY_____ STATE_____ ZIP_____

Silhouette Romance

IT'S YOUR OWN SPECIAL TIME

Contemporary romances for today's women.
Each month, six very special love stories will be yours
from SILHOUETTE. Look for them wherever books are sold
or order now from the coupon below.

$1.50 each

☐ 5 Goforth	☐ 28 Hampson	☐ 54 Beckman	☐ 83 Halston
☐ 6 Stanford	☐ 29 Wildman	☐ 55 LaDame	☐ 84 Vitek
☐ 7 Lewis	☐ 30 Dixon	☐ 56 Trent	☐ 85 John
☐ 8 Beckman	☐ 32 Michaels	☐ 57 John	☐ 86 Adams
☐ 9 Wilson	☐ 33 Vitek	☐ 58 Stanford	☐ 87 Michaels
☐ 10 Caine	☐ 34 John	☐ 59 Vernon	☐ 88 Stanford
☐ 11 Vernon	☐ 35 Stanford	☐ 60 Hill	☐ 89 James
☐ 17 John	☐ 38 Browning	☐ 61 Michaels	☐ 90 Major
☐ 19 Thornton	☐ 39 Sinclair	☐ 62 Halston	☐ 92 McKay
☐ 20 Fulford	☐ 46 Stanford	☐ 63 Brent	☐ 93 Browning
☐ 22 Stephens	☐ 47 Vitek	☐ 71 Ripy	☐ 94 Hampson
☐ 23 Edwards	☐ 48 Wildman	☐ 73 Browning	☐ 95 Wisdom
☐ 24 Healy	☐ 49 Wisdom	☐ 76 Hardy	☐ 96 Beckman
☐ 25 Stanford	☐ 50 Scott	☐ 78 Oliver	☐ 97 Clay
☐ 26 Hastings	☐ 52 Hampson	☐ 81 Roberts	☐ 98 St. George
☐ 27 Hampson	☐ 53 Browning	☐ 82 Dailey	☐ 99 Camp

$1.75 each

☐ 100 Stanford	☐ 114 Michaels	☐ 128 Hampson	☐ 143 Roberts
☐ 101 Hardy	☐ 115 John	☐ 129 Converse	☐ 144 Goforth
☐ 102 Hastings	☐ 116 Lindley	☐ 130 Hardy	☐ 145 Hope
☐ 103 Cork	☐ 117 Scott	☐ 131 Stanford	☐ 146 Michaels
☐ 104 Vitek	☐ 118 Dailey	☐ 132 Wisdom	☐ 147 Hampson
☐ 105 Eden	☐ 119 Hampson	☐ 133 Rowe	☐ 148 Cork
☐ 106 Dailey	☐ 120 Carroll	☐ 134 Charles	☐ 149 Saunders
☐ 107 Bright	☐ 121 Langan	☐ 135 Logan	☐ 150 Major
☐ 108 Hampson	☐ 122 Scofield	☐ 136 Hampson	☐ 151 Hampson
☐ 109 Vernon	☐ 123 Sinclair	☐ 137 Hunter	☐ 152 Halston
☐ 110 Trent	☐ 124 Beckman	☐ 138 Wilson	☐ 153 Dailey
☐ 111 South	☐ 125 Bright	☐ 139 Vitek	☐ 154 Beckman
☐ 112 Stanford	☐ 126 St. George	☐ 140 Erskine	☐ 155 Hampson
☐ 113 Browning	☐ 127 Roberts	☐ 142 Browning	☐ 156 Sawyer

Love, passion and adventure will be yours FREE for 15 days... with Tapestry™ historical romances!

"Long before women could read and write, tapestries were used to record events and stories . . . especially the exploits of courageous knights and their ladies."

And now there's a new kind of tapestry...

In the pages of Tapestry™ romance novels, you'll find love, intrigue, and historical touches that really make the stories come alive!

You'll meet brave Guyon d'Arcy, a Norman knight . . . handsome Comte Andre de Crillon, a Huguenot royalist . . . rugged Branch Taggart, a feuding American rancher . . . and more. And on each journey back in time, you'll experience tender romance and searing passion . . . and learn about the way people lived and loved in earlier times than ours.

We think you'll be so delighted with Tapestry romances, you won't want to miss a single one! We'd like to send you 2 books each month, as soon as they are published, through our Tapestry Home Subscription Service.℠ Look them over for 15 days, free. If not delighted, simply return them and owe nothing. But if you enjoy them as much as we think you will, pay the invoice enclosed. There's never any additional charge for this convenient service — we pay all postage and handling costs.

To receive your Tapestry historical romances, fill out the coupon below and mail it to us today. You're on your way to all the love, passion, and adventure of times gone by!

HISTORICAL *Tapestry* ROMANCES

Tapestry™ is a trademark of Simon & Schuster.

Silhouette Desire
15-Day Trial Offer
A new romance series that explores contemporary relationships in exciting detail

Six Silhouette Desire romances, free for 15 days!
We'll send you six new Silhouette Desire romances to look over for 15 days, absolutely free! If you decide not to keep the books, return them and owe nothing.

Six books a month, free home delivery. If you like Silhouette Desire romances as much as we think you will, keep them and return your payment with the invoice. Then we will send you six new books every month to preview, just as soon as they are published. You pay only for the books you decide to keep, and you never pay postage and handling.